THE GATES OF PARADISE

Narina went to her room and stood at the window looking out towards the sea.

She was thinking how bizarre it all was.

In a twinkling of an eye she had been transmitted from her quiet home in Hertfordshire to this strange land, where the local people were striving against being overrun by their greedy and aggressive neighbour.

'They are small,' she mused, 'and very vulnerable. Is it really possible that the Union Jack in the shape of the wife of the ruling Prince can possibly save them?'

Then it was as if the answer to her question came to her straight from Heaven.

She realised that whatever the cost, Louise, and all those who were so proud of being British would stand and fight – they would defy the enemy and never give in.

Looking up at the sky as the sunshine was turning the garden into a fairyland of intense beauty, Narina prayed that she would play her part, however small, perfectly and without fault –

That God would give her the strength and resilience that Alexanderburg so desperately needed.

THE BARBARA CARTLAND PINK COLLECTION

Titles in this series

1. The Cross Of Love
2. Love In The Highlands
3. Love Finds The Way
4. The Castle Of Love
5. Love Is Triumphant
6. Stars In The Sky
7. The Ship Of Love
8. A Dangerous Disguise
9. Love Became Theirs
10. Love Drives In
11. Sailing To Love
12. The Star Of Love
13. Music Is The Soul Of Love
14. Love In The East
15. Theirs To Eternity
16. A Paradise On Earth
17. Love Wins In Berlin
18. In Search Of Love
19. Love Rescues Rosanna
20. A Heart In Heaven
21. The House Of Happiness
22. Royalty Defeated By Love
23. The White Witch
24. They Sought Love
25. Love Is The Reason For Living
26. They Found Their Way To Heaven
27. Learning To Love
28. Journey To Happiness
29. A Kiss In The Desert
30. The Heart Of Love
31. The Richness Of Love
32. For Ever And Ever
33. An Unexpected Love
34. Saved By An Angel
35. Touching The Stars
36. Seeking Love
37. Journey To Love
38. The Importance Of Love
39. Love By The Lake
40. A Dream Come True
41. The King Without A Heart
42. The Waters Of Love
43. Danger To The Duke
44. A Perfect Way To Heaven
45. Follow Your Heart
46. In Hiding
47. Rivals For Love
48. A Kiss From The Heart
49. Lovers In London
50. This Way To Heaven
51. A Princess Prays
52. Mine For Ever
53. The Earl's Revenge
54. Love At The Tower
55. Ruled By Love
56. Love Came From Heaven
57. Love And Apollo
58. The Keys Of Love
59. A Castle Of Dreams
60. A Battle Of Brains
61. A Change Of Hearts
62. It Is Love
63. The Triumph Of Love
64. Wanted – A Royal Wife
65. A Kiss Of Love
66. To Heaven With Love
67. Pray For Love
68. The Marquis Is Trapped
69. Hide And Seek For Love
70. Hiding From Love
71. A Teacher Of Love
72. Money Or Love
73. The Revelation Is Love
74. The Tree Of Love
75. The Magnificent Marquis
76. The Castle
77. The Gates Of Paradise

THE GATES OF PARADISE

BARBARA CARTLAND

Barbaracartland.com Ltd

First published on the internet in February 2011
by Barbaracartland.com

ISBN 978-1-906950-26-2

The characters and situations in this book are entirely imaginary and bear no relation to any real person or actual happening.

Printed and bound in Great Britain by Cle-Print Ltd.
of St Ives, Cambridgeshire.

THE BARBARA CARTLAND PINK COLLECTION

Barbara Cartland was the most prolific bestselling author in the history of the world. She was frequently in the Guinness Book of Records for writing more books in a year than any other living author. In fact her most amazing literary feat was when her publishers asked for more Barbara Cartland romances, she doubled her output from 10 books a year to over 20 books a year, when she was 77.

She went on writing continuously at this rate for 20 years and wrote her last book at the age of 97, thus completing 400 books between the ages of 77 and 97.

Her publishers finally could not keep up with this phenomenal output, so at her death she left 160 unpublished manuscripts, something again that no other author has ever achieved.

Now the exciting news is that these 160 original unpublished Barbara Cartland books are already being published and by Barbaracartland.com exclusively on the internet, as the international web is the best possible way of reaching so many Barbara Cartland readers around the world.

The 160 books are published monthly and will be numbered in sequence.

The series is called the Pink Collection as a tribute to Barbara Cartland whose favourite colour was pink and it became very much her trademark over the years.

The Barbara Cartland Pink Collection is published only on the internet. Log on to www.barbaracartland.com to find out how you can purchase the books monthly as they are published, and take out a subscription that will ensure that all subsequent editions are delivered to you by mail order to your home.

NEW

Barbaracartland.com is proud to announce the publication of ten new Audio Books for the first time as CDs. They are favourite Barbara Cartland stories read by well-known actors and actresses and each story extends to 4 or 5 CDs. The Audio Books are as follows:

The Patient Bridegroom	The Passion and the Flower
A Challenge of Hearts	Little White Doves of Love
A Train to Love	The Prince and the Pekinese
The Unbroken Dream	A King in Love
The Cruel Count	A Sign of Love

More Audio Books will be published in the future and the above titles can be purchased by logging on to the website www.barbaracartland.com or please write to the address below.

If you do not have access to a computer, you can write for information about the Barbara Cartland Pink Collection and the Barbara Cartland Audio Books to the following address:

Barbara Cartland.com Ltd., Camfield Place,
Hatfield, Hertfordshire AL9 6JE, United Kingdom.

Telephone: +44 (0)1707 642629
Fax: +44 (0)1707 663041

THE LATE DAME BARBARA CARTLAND

Barbara Cartland who sadly died in May 2000 at the age of nearly 99 was the world's most famous romantic novelist who wrote 723 books in her lifetime with worldwide sales of over 1 billion copies and her books were translated into 36 different languages.

As well as romantic novels, she wrote historical biographies, 6 autobiographies, theatrical plays, books of advice on life, love, vitamins and cookery. She also found time to be a political speaker and television and radio personality.

She wrote her first book at the age of 21 and this was called *Jigsaw*. It became an immediate bestseller and sold 100,000 copies in hardback and was translated into 6 different languages. She wrote continuously throughout her life, writing bestsellers for an astonishing 76 years. Her books have always been immensely popular in the United States, where in 1976 her current books were at numbers 1 & 2 in the B. Dalton bestsellers list, a feat never achieved before or since by any author.

Barbara Cartland became a legend in her own lifetime and will be best remembered for her wonderful romantic novels, so loved by her millions of readers throughout the world.

Her books will always be treasured for their moral message, her pure and innocent heroines, her good looking and dashing heroes and above all her belief that the power of love is more important than anything else in everyone's life.

"Paradise is a place we would all love to find, but perfection can easily masquerade as an illusion. Paradise for me has always been to be adored and cherished by a wonderful man who has conquered my heart and my soul absolutely."

Barbara Cartland

CHAPTER ONE
1880

Narina tore open the letter with a strange stamp that had just been delivered and gave a cry of excitement.

She read it through twice carefully in order to be quite certain she had not made a mistake.

Then she ran down the passage towards her father's study.

The Very Right Reverend John Kenwin, Bishop of St. Albans, was busy composing his sermon for the next day, which was Palm Sunday.

He was a good-looking man with a deep voice that captivated every member of his congregation.

The third son of a distinguished Statesman, he had gone into the Church as it was traditional in his family.

He had an outstanding intellect and together with his irresistible charm, he rose rapidly to become a Bishop just after he was fifty, and it was already taken for granted that he would be the next Archbishop of Canterbury.

His father, Lord Kenwin, had behaved traditionally with all his three sons.

The eldest son had gone into the Life Guards as had a great number of his family before him and he had then been transferred to Windsor Castle.

There he not only guarded Queen Victoria but was someone whose advice she often sought.

He married one of Her Majesty's ladies-in-waiting and now that he was approaching the age of retirement he was a highly respected member of her Household.

The second son of Lord Kenwin had gone into the Navy, where he enjoyed the chance it gave him of seeing the world and had recently been promoted Admiral.

With such an impressive family background it was not surprising that Narina was exceedingly intelligent.

She had left her school with a prize for practically every subject she had been interested in.

In addition to her brain she was also outstandingly beautiful.

It was not only the beauty of her features that were almost classical in their perfection.

The expression in her eyes was enchanting and her charming manner she had inherited from her father.

When she reached the study door she opened it very carefully.

She peeped in to see if he was alone and as he was she went in.

Moving quietly up to him she put her hands on his shoulders and bent over to kiss his cheek.

"Oh, it is you, Narina!" he exclaimed.

"Who else did you think was kissing you, Papa?"

He smiled at her.

"You know I am busy with my sermon."

"Yes, Papa, but I really had to interrupt you to tell you about this exciting letter I have just received."

Her father sat back in his chair, realising it must be important or his daughter would not have bothered him.

"It has come by Special Messenger from London, and who do you think it is from?"

"I am not going to guess," he replied, "because, as you can see, I am very busy."

"Then I will tell you. It is from Louise – Princess Louise, now reigning in Alexanderburg."

"I remember her well, a very pretty girl and I know she was your greatest friend at school."

"I love her dearly and because we are remarkably alike, we were always together and the teachers called us '*the twins*'."

"And you have just heard from her, Narina?"

He knew that if she started reminiscing about her friend Louise, he would not be able to finish his sermon.

"I have not heard from Louise for quite some time, and now she has written to me saying it is very urgent and if I love her, I must join her *at once* in Alexanderburg."

The Bishop looked surprised.

"Join her at once, Narina?"

"Yes. She did not say why, but just wrote that she needs me and feels certain that I will not fail her."

"She must have some good reason for begging you to go to her at what one might say is a moment's notice."

Narina gave a little laugh.

"Louise was always impetuous, and if she wanted something or someone it was always 'immediately'. But this really does sound urgent."

"How does she expect you to go there?"

"That apparently has been arranged. A letter came with hers from their Embassy in London saying that on Princess Louise's instructions a Battleship would pick me up at Tilbury and take me to Alexanderburg."

"A Battleship!" her Papa exclaimed in amazement.

"I suppose a Battleship is faster than other ships – "

"For such a long journey it could not be better and of course, my dearest, you want to go?"

"Of course I do, Papa, to tell the truth I was a little surprised that Louise did not send for me before. We were so close at the school and when we were both *debutantes*, we attended the same balls every night."

"I well remember, Narina, but to be honest I always felt that my own daughter was the most beautiful of the two."

She gave him a flashing smile.

"Thank you, Papa, that is exactly what I want you to say. Equally you must understand that if Louise really needs me, as she says she does, I feel I must go to her."

"Then you should definitely go, my dear, it will be a good experience for you to see a part of the world which I unfortunately have not visited myself. But I have always been interested in the Balkans, and I would have enjoyed sailing through the Dardanelles and into the Black Sea."

Narina gave a little cry of excitement.

"Yes, yes, and it will be very thrilling."

"We will look at it on the map tonight, but for the moment, I suggest, if the messenger is waiting as I expect he is, that you tell him how soon you will be ready to join the Battleship at Tilbury.

"I presume they are arranging for both a chaperone and a Guardian to look after you?"

"Yes, yes, Papa. Louise says in the postscript,"

"*I have arranged for a charming couple from our Embassy to be in attendance on you and they will provide you with a maid to look after you whilst you are at sea.*"

"It does seem to me, Narina, that your friend, the Princess, has thought of everything. Thus, my dear, write and tell her how soon you can embark and, as it seems to be urgent, you must not keep her waiting too long."

"I just that knew you would understand, Papa, and I only wish that you were coming with me."

"I just wish I could – there is nothing I would enjoy more, but as you know, I have a mass of engagements that are quite impossible to cancel."

"I am being greedy and asking for too much, Papa, but I would have really loved to have you tell me in your own way about all the places I shall pass as I sail across the Mediterranean and up the Aegean Sea."

As she finished speaking, the Bishop then realised that his daughter was not waiting for his answer.

She had moved towards the door.

"I will tell them that I will embark on Tuesday as that will give me time to buy anything extra I will require."

She was gone before he could agree or disagree, so he gave a little sigh and turned once again to his sermon.

*

For the next two days Narina was in a wild state of excitement.

It was not just the thought of the voyage ahead that thrilled her for she loved travelling, but she was so looking forward to seeing her friend again.

She had missed Louise overwhelmingly ever since she had married.

It had been an arranged marriage – Louise was the daughter of Princess Beatrice whose mother was a second cousin to Queen Victoria.

The Queen was very often called '*the Matchmaker of Europe*' as she had provided a great number of her close relations to be the wives of Rulers in the Balkans.

It was no secret that the Russians were determined to enlarge their Empire which was already enormous and to do so they had begun taking over many small Principalities attached to Austria, Moldavia and Rumania. Besides these there was the temptation of the even smaller Principalities of Bosnia, Serbia and Eastern Roumelia.

They were very devious about it, finding out where the Ruler was weak or too old to competently carry on, so they then provoked rebellions and intervened claiming that they must move in to ensure peace.

The only countries they dared not touch were those that were entitled to fly the Union Jack.

Queen Victoria was therefore always beseeched by diplomats, begging her to send a British Royal wife for the protection of the reigning Prince or King.

Only Her Majesty, they assured her, could preserve their country against the aggressive Russians.

Apart from this, as the British were well aware, the Russian Cossacks were spreading out over Asia, gobbling up Caravan towns and Khanates and thus shortening the miles between Russia and India.

Narina had heard all this from her Papa, but she had not been in the slightest worried about her friend Louise.

She had been fortunate in her arranged marriage.

As she had told Narina in the first letter she wrote, her husband was a charming and delightful ruling Prince and she had fallen in love with him at first sight.

"*I never expected,*" she explained to Narina, "*to be as happy as I am with Rudolf or to enjoy every moment of my life as I do now.*"

Narina had been delighted and reassured.

It had been impossible for Prince Rudolf to leave his country and come to England and so Louise had been married in Alexanderburg without Narina as bridesmaid.

They had planned when they talked about marriage at their school that they would be bridesmaid to each other, while the one who married first would be matron of honour to the other.

They had imagined that their weddings would take place in one of the great Cathedrals near their homes.

When they walked up the aisle, it would be with at least eight or ten bridesmaids with the chief bridesmaid, of course, being either Louise or Narina.

But Queen Victoria had sent for Louise and told her that she was to marry Prince Rudolf of Alexanderburg.

"I just cannot believe it," Louise had said when she returned from Windsor Castle. "I thought that I must be imagining what Her Majesty said to me. But naturally I could not possibly refuse such an incredible honour and my Mama keeps telling me how lucky I am."

Narina, however, had shed more than a few tears when she kissed Louise goodbye.

Accompanied by her mother, Princess Beatrice, and at least a dozen other relatives, she had slipped away on an English Battleship to Alexanderburg.

Narina had worried about her friend to begin with, but then she had received Louise's letters telling her how blissfully happy she was at Alexanderburg and that Prince Rudolf really was the man of her dreams.

Then after a year had passed by and the letters from Louise grew fewer month by month – she wrote very little about her marriage, although she still seemed to be happy.

Now Narina calculated she must have been married for over two years.

In the meantime she herself had received several proposals of marriage, but they were not from anyone she loved or had any wish to marry.

She was intelligent enough to recognise that Louise had been extremely lucky.

She had indeed found the man of her dreams in an 'arranged marriage', while she herself had not met anyone with whom she wished to spend the rest of her life.

She was in fact exceedingly happy with her father and she had been kept very busy with his affairs, as he was constantly moving from one appointment to another.

Then he was consecrated Bishop of St. Albans.

Narina felt certain that they would stay there until he was promoted, as she hoped, to Canterbury.

Fortunately her grandfather's house was situated in Hertfordshire as well, and she had therefore found a great many friends who had been fond of her mother and many girls and boys she had known when she was a child.

She certainly did not lack for invitations and there were parties and entertainments of every sort taking place week after week.

Even so she still missed Louise.

Although Narina wrote to her every week, as they had done when she first married, she was a little hurt that Louise's replies came so spasmodically.

They were not, she thought, as intimate as they had been when she had first left England.

Now this idea of travelling out to her because she was needed was something enthralling.

Narina found it difficult to concentrate properly on what she should take with her to wear and then there were presents to be bought for Louise and her Prince.

She also thought it would be a mistake not to take a selection of the latest books with her as her father thought that they would be of interest to Prince Rudolf.

The hours passed by, it seemed to Narina, with a swiftness that left her breathless.

*

Finally early on Tuesday morning she and her Papa drove off to London.

She was sure as they did so that they had left half the items she would need behind.

"Do not worry about it," he counselled, "as far as I remember, you and Louise were always exchanging your clothes when you were young and I don't expect that either of you will have altered much in the last two years!"

Narina laughed.

"That is quite true, Papa. I remember being furious with Louise when she succeeded in ruining my best dress by spilling coffee on it! While she accused me of spoiling her best hat when it blew off my head in a wind!"

"I only remember how pretty you two girls were and how much I enjoyed having Louise to stay with us."

"I always believed, Papa, that she loved you better than she loved her own father, but I was far too tactful to say so."

"You were right to keep those feelings to yourself, and Princess Beatrice was a most charming woman and it is only a pity she is not still with us today."

Actually the Princess had died only a year after her daughter married and Narina had written to Louise to tell her how sorry she was.

But today she certainly did not want to remember the sad times – only the happy ones.

In fact she was feeling quite sure that Louise was not sending for her because she was unhappy.

In her last letter she had told Narina what fun she and her husband had when bathing in the Black Sea, where they had built a small Summer Palace in a quiet bay some way along the coast from the Capital of Alexenderburg.

They could easily escape to this idyllic spot and be

on their own without too many courtiers and all the pomp and ceremony of the Court.

Nevertheless when she had retired to her bed in the comfortable cabin she had been given in the Battleship, she found herself wondering over and over again why Louise needed her so urgently.

Her father had been somewhat surprised at how few attendants there were to accompany his daughter on her journey to Alexanderburg.

There was only Baron Von Graben and his wife.

The Baroness was much younger than her husband and she was most attractive like most Austrian women.

She always enjoyed travelling with her husband on his diplomatic missions, mostly because she was invariably pursued by the men of any country they were visiting.

She enjoyed dancing more than any other activity and the Baron said he was too old to dance, but he had the reputation of being an extremely able diplomat.

He was also a master of many different languages and boasted he could speak with most other diplomats in their own language.

Besides the Baron and Baroness there was nobody else except an Austrian maid, who was to look after Narina as well as the Baroness.

Narina knew that her Papa was surprised at such a small party, but he was too courteous to comment.

"One thing, my dearest," he whispered to Narina when they were alone in her cabin, "you will be able to rest before you arrive and enjoy the books I have given you."

He had provided her with four books about Russia and the Balkan States from his extensive library.

"It is always a good idea," he advised her, "to learn as much as possible about any country you are visiting – otherwise you might miss something of significance."

"You have told me that before, Papa, and as you know, I have always tried to carry out your instructions."

"Well my instructions are for you to read all these books. They will tell you about the people, their religions, their superstitions and above all their aspirations."

The Bishop looked over his shoulder to make quite certain that there was no one listening.

"Be careful," he said. "The Russians are being very difficult in the Balkans, as Her Majesty was saying to me last week, they are taking over far too many Principalities. In fact Her Majesty is most worried about the situation."

"I realise that, Papa, and I will be very careful what I say. At the same time it must be worrying for Louise."

"I am quite sure that Alexanderburg is safe as long as she is still on the throne – "

"She did not mention any trouble in her letters, but sadly there have not been so many letters recently."

"I am sure she has a good reason for asking you to go," the Bishop reflected, "and you must help her in every way you can."

He paused, thinking just how Queen Victoria had expressed her anger to him at the Russians' behaviour.

"If I had not sent my Battleships into the Aegean Sea," she had raged, "those Russians would have been in Constantinople by now. Heaven knows how hard I had to fight the Prime Minister to get him to pay any attention!"

"But you definitely saved Constantinople, ma'am," the Bishop added.

He was recalling how the Grand Duke Nicholas had been forced to turn back when his Army was only six miles from Constantinople, but it had cost him the loss of twenty thousand men making it quite impossible for the Russians to defy Great Britain again.

It occurred to the Bishop, as he mused about it, that perhaps Narina was heading into danger and then he told himself he was being unnecessarily perturbed by the idea.

For as long as the British flag was flying high over Alexanderburg, the Russians would not dare to intervene.

He put his arms round Narina,

"Goodbye, my dearest. I know that you will help your friend Louise and it will be delightful for you to be together again. At the same time do not forget your Papa."

"As though I could, Papa. I love you and I shall miss our conversations and all your stories that are always so enthralling."

She kissed her father.

"Store them all up for when I return home. Then I will appreciate your wisdom all the more."

He chuckled and then held her close and kissed her affectionately.

"I love you, my dearest Narina, and I will pray that God will bless your visit and that you will be able to help Princess Louise as you wish to do."

"Yes, do not forget me in your prayers, Papa, and I will pray for you in mine as well."

She went up on deck and as the Battleship moved slowly away, she waved until her father was out of sight.

Then she went below to help the maid unpack the clothes she would need while they were at sea and to hang them up in the cupboards in her cabin.

The maid could speak reasonably good English, but Narina talked to her in German which delighted her.

Then once the Battleship was moving more quickly she went to find the Baron and Baroness.

They were seated in the cabin which adjoined the Captain's.

The Baroness was already complaining that the sea was rough, although there was as yet very little movement.

Narina was sure that when they reached the Bay of Biscay, she would retire to her cabin and not be seen again until the end of the voyage.

This proved to be an accurate forecast!

Narina, however, was soon to find the compliments the Baron kept paying her rather embarrassing.

As she was a Clergyman's daughter, it often made people over-polite and she found they were inclined to treat her differently from the way they treated other girls.

They all expected her to be shocked at the slightest thing and they did not overwhelm her with compliments on her beauty or the way she was dressed.

She was well aware, and it rather amused her, that the men thought it was in some way unfitting, as her father was in the Church, for her to be so outstandingly pretty.

In fact if they did pay her a compliment, they would begin by saying,

"I daresay your father would think it improper for me to say this to you, Narina, but you are undoubtedly the most beautiful girl here tonight."

When she told her father what had been said to her, he had merely grinned.

"I seem to put a curb on their turning your head too quickly, but I agree with them, you are much prettier than any of your contemporaries. But I promise that I will not rebuke them for being truthful in saying so!"

"Of course you wouldn't, Papa, but I am only afraid that I might be missing something."

"I think you will be told a great number of times by many men that you are very lovely, and I remember when I first married your mother, she told me that men used to say to her, 'I am longing to flirt with you, Mrs. Kenwin, but I am terrified your husband might put a curse on me'!"

Narina thought this was hilarious.

"And did you, Papa?"

He shook his head.

"I had no need to do so. Your mother and I fell in love with each other the moment we met, it was impossible for either of us ever to find anyone else attractive."

Narina always believed that every house they lived in, wherever it was, was filled with love and the sun always seemed to shine.

It was the sublime love she wanted for herself, but she was only afraid that it would never happen to her.

Certainly the men she had met seemed somewhat dull and rather ineffective compared to her beloved father, and although she enjoyed dancing with them they had very little else to offer her.

Her father had never seemed to be worried, as her mother had, about her getting married.

And in fact he had said more than once,

"There is no hurry for you to be married and as we are so happy together there is no point yet in your thinking of yourself as an 'old maid'!"

Narina had giggled.

"I certainly don't do that! It is only when the girls who came out at the same time as me get married that I begin to feel a little that I am being left behind."

"There is no hurry about love," her father advised. "It will come to you one day out of the blue and it will be the right sort of love we all seek in our hearts and some of us are privileged to find."

"As you did, Papa."

"As I did. I know that your mother and I will meet again when I join her in Heaven, and I am quite certain she is listening to us both now, knowing that what I am telling you is the truth and there is no need for you to hurry."

Narina had kissed him.

"As long as I have you, Papa, I have no wish to be with anyone else."

This was true.

Nevertheless when she was alone, she often wished that there was someone to share her interests – most of all someone to ride with her when Papa was unable to do so.

Now as the ship was moving out into the open sea she was thinking just how superb it would be if he could be with her.

He would tell her, as he always did, stories which other people did not know about the countries they were passing, especially those bordering the Mediterranean.

There was so much more she wanted to know about Africa and especially Greece.

Her Papa had been entranced when he was a young man by the wonder and beauty of Ancient Greece and she had learnt the language from him.

She had thought one day she would like to go with someone she loved to Delphi and its shimmering cliffs and visit the Greek Islands, especially Delos where Apollo was born.

"Every girl," her Papa had said once, "would like the man she marries to look like Apollo. But I have found that handsome men do not always make good husbands."

"Why not, Papa?" she asked quizzically.

"Because they are more concerned with their own looks than those of their wives. And if there is to be one beautiful person in the family, it should be the woman."

"Why, Papa?" Narina persisted.

"If you have a husband who is too handsome, you will be fighting very hard to protect and keep him, instead of him fighting to protect *you* from being swept away!"

It was just the sort of joke Papa would make and Narina laughed.

But she learnt as she watched her contemporaries that he was right and she had told herself there was no need to pray for Apollo as her husband, but a man who would adore her and fight off any who tried to take her from him.

At the moment, however, there had been no one for whom she had felt the least affection.

Anyway it was not affection she wanted, but love – the overwhelming love so beautifully described in books she had read and it was, she was quite certain, what women all over the world were always seeking.

'Perhaps some are just unlucky,' she mused.

However, it was very seldom that she worried about acquiring admirers.

There would be no one on the Battleship, she felt, who would pay her any compliments.

But to her surprise she was mistaken.

As she expected, the Baroness retired to her cabin and was not seen again on the voyage and the Baron, when they were alone, plied her with compliments!

He looked at her with his aging eyes in a way that made her feel somewhat embarrassed.

If it had not been from a man of his age, she might have felt shy, instead of which she found herself sparring with the Baron in words, being in a way somewhat rude to him, but equally she was aware that he must have been a *roué* in his youth.

It was impossible for him to be alone with a pretty woman and not flirt with her.

As the Battleship steamed down the Mediterranean and into the Aegean Sea, she found the Baron's incessant compliments increasingly boring.

And she was aware that when she was near him, his hands would automatically come out to try and touch her.

It became quite a game for her to avoid him, but it was a bit difficult in the rather cramped circumstances of the Battleship.

They sat opposite each other at meals, but while he could not touch her with his hands, his eyes were always on her face and the compliments would come blithely from his tongue in a number of different languages.

Narina especially enjoyed practising the language of Alexanderburg, which she found was an easily picked up dialect of German, in order to answer the Baron back.

Occasionally she would defeat him by a riposte that made them both laugh.

"If I was a bit younger," the Baron said in his rather thick voice, "I would hold you tightly in my arms so that you could not escape me and then kiss you until we were both breathless!"

"And if I was younger," Narina managed to retort, "I would doubtless appreciate it because I would not know better. But now I have become very discriminating and I am sure you have no wish to fail at a game at which at one time you must have been a past master!"

The Baron threw back his head and laughed, but he did not cease to ply her with compliments.

She was unsure if he might wish to pursue her after she had retired, so she was therefore always very careful to lock her cabin door.

'No one would ever believe it was necessary,' she reflected. 'But one never knows and it is a mistake to be wise after the event.'

As they moved up the Dardanelles, Narina became more and more excited.

Now she was certain that once she was with Louise again they would be as happy as they had been when they were at school together.

The Battleship sailed through the Sea of Marmara and then up the Bosporus.

When they eventually reached the Black Sea, the sun was shining brightly and it was really too hot to be on deck without a hat or a sunshade.

They were steaming, Narina was sure, at what must be record speed and she was wondering why the Captain had not stopped at any port on the way.

She had longed to spend just a few hours in Athens or spend an hour on one of the Greek Islands.

But the engines did not stop rolling.

At last she could see the coast of Alexanderburg in the distance.

It was then she was certain there was some special reason why they must reach Louise as quickly as possible.

Then when she assumed that they would soon dock at the Port of Balchik, the engines slowed down and to her astonishment, almost out of sight of land, they finally came to a stop.

"What has happened? What has gone wrong?" she asked.

Because she was so surprised and anxious, she ran along the deck and climbed up onto the bridge.

"What on earth has happened?" she rather sharply demanded of the Captain. "Why have we stopped here?"

"We will be moving in as soon as it is dark," the Captain replied. "Actually, Miss Kenwin, I have arrived slightly sooner than I had anticipated."

"But why do we have to wait until it is dark?"

"Those are my orders, and you will be taken ashore as soon as the boat comes for you."

There was a short pause and then Narina said in a puzzled voice,

"You said *I* would be taken ashore. What about the Baron and Baroness?"

"I will be taking them both back to Constantinople where the Baron is now to be posted," replied the Captain.

Narina was astonished. The Baron had never once mentioned that his destination was Constantinople and not Alexanderburg.

She could understand that he and his wife had been asked to chaperone her on the voyage and yet it seemed so strange that he had not told her about his plans.

Nor had he said amongst his other overwhelming compliments that he would miss her when she left them.

She had in fact thought he would be living near the Palace and they would meet again after she joined Louise.

It was very obvious, however, that the Captain did not want to answer any more questions and Narina thought, although it might be her imagination, that he was rather embarrassed by her reaction.

She knew that the Capital of Alexanderburg was on the coast and the Palace was just outside the City. She had been told by Louise in one of her letters that it was high up on a hill.

At least they were there.

Yet it seemed as every minute passed by more and more extraordinary that she was not allowed to go ashore.

Finally the sun disappeared below the horizon and darkness fell quickly.

Her luggage was packed and had been taken up on deck, but still they waited and waited.

Eventually when the stars were coming out one by one and the moon was climbing up the sky, she saw a boat.

It was quite a large one with a hood over the stern and it was coming towards them.

It was then that the Baron came on deck and stood beside her.

"I shall miss you, my lovely and beautiful English rose," he murmured.

"I thought you were coming to Alexanderburg too," Narina quizzed him. "You did not tell me you were going to Constantinople."

"I just wish I could be with you and I will miss you more than I can possibly say," the Baron responded. "But my duty calls and I have actually overstayed my leave by coming here with you."

"Then I must thank you very much for doing so."

"I must thank you too, Miss Kerwin, for making me feel young again and entranced as I have not been for many years by anything so exquisite and perfect as your lips."

Because he was speaking in French it seemed not so embarrassing as if he had been speaking in English.

Narina looked away from him.

"One day," the Baron continued quietly, "you will be kissed as you ought to be kissed, and I am only envious of the man who will do it. I do wish, as I have wished ever since this voyage began, that I was thirty years younger."

"You have been very kind to me," Narina managed to say, "and thank you for all you have done. I hope what you are going to do in Constantinople will be a success."

"It will be," replied the Baron. "But tonight I shall think of you and dream that you are in my arms."

Before she could reply, the Captain was beside her.

"The boat is ready for you, Miss Kenwin," he said, "and I hope that you have enjoyed your voyage."

"More than I could say, Captain, and thank you for all your kindness. I will always remember how delightful this voyage has been."

She held out her hand to the Baron who kissed it and then she followed the Captain below to the gangway and into the small boat bobbing beside the Battleship.

Then as the boat moved away quickly, to Narina's surprise, there was no one in it to greet her.

She rose to her feet and waved briskly to the Baron who was leaning over the rail on deck. She could just see his raised arm and then it was too dark to see any more.

She sat down on the seat in the stern wondering as she had wondered before why she was taken ashore in this strange manner.

What could possibly be waiting for her when she arrived in Alexanderburg?

CHAPTER TWO

When the boat came to a standstill, Narina realised that they were now against a quay and the sailors who had been rowing the boat shipped their oars.

Next someone came out of the shadows to help her ashore.

She wanted to ask who the man was and if he had come from the Palace.

As he said nothing, she had a strange feeling that she too should be silent.

No one else spoke and the man walked ahead and she followed him to the end of the quay.

Then she saw what was obviously a Royal carriage waiting for her. It had the Royal Arms emblazoned on its side and was drawn by two horses.

The door was open and still without a word being spoken she stepped into the carriage.

As the carriage drove off, she thought the situation was turning stranger and stranger.

In fact she was becoming rather apprehensive.

It did not seem at all like Louise or the way she and her Papa would have behaved if someone was coming to stay with them.

Now there were a number of dim street lights and she noticed a few people walking about.

She had read in her books that Balchik, the Capital

of Alexanderburg, was a bustling and prosperous City, but it was impossible to see much through the glass windows.

After driving for nearly twenty minutes she realised that the carriage was going uphill and then she remembered that the Palace overlooked the City.

On and on they drove until she saw that they were passing through an imposing gateway guarded by sentries who presented arms as she passed.

Now she must be within the Palace grounds, but she could only see trees against the sky.

When finally the Palace came into sight it was quite impossible even in the moonlight to see it at all clearly.

At last the carriage came to a standstill.

Then as the carriage door opened, she was aware that a tall grey-haired man was waiting to greet her.

As she reached him, he held out his hand,

"Welcome to Alexanderburg, Miss Kenwin, and I am very grateful to you for coming."

He spoke, she thought, in a low voice and when she was about to reply, he added,

"Please follow me, and it is best if we say nothing until we reach Her Royal Highness."

Narina found this extraordinary and equally it was rather unnerving.

She had not really expected Louise, now she was a Princess, to meet her on the doorstep and yet she knew it was something she would always have done instinctively.

The grey-haired man who had welcomed her was now walking quickly along a narrow undecorated passage and up what appeared to be back staircase.

As they reached the top he opened a door and much to Narina's relief she saw there were bright lights.

Now she could see that she was in a very large and impressive corridor with gilt-framed pictures on the walls and some exquisite inlaid cabinets beneath them.

For a moment she could only look around her and then she turned to the man who had led her up the stairs.

He looked, she now thought, very distinguished.

Almost as if she had asked the question, he said,

"Allow me to introduce myself, Miss Kenwin, I am Count Franz Klaus, the Lord Chamberlain to His Royal Highness Prince Rudolf."

Narina, not knowing what she should say, smiled at him shyly.

"I am very grateful indeed," the Lord Chamberlain went on, "that you have come here so quickly and now I will take you to see Her Royal Highness who is waiting for you impatiently."

This was just what Narina wanted to hear.

She then followed the Lord Chamberlain eagerly as he walked down the corridor and turned into another one, before he stopped by some double doors.

The Lord Chamberlain knocked on the doors three times and instantly the doors were opened from inside and again he walked in first with Narina following him.

They were now walking swiftly down a brilliantly lit corridor that widened out until she could see the doors of several rooms opening out from it.

The Lord Chamberlain went to the centre room and as he opened the door, Narina gave a cry.

Standing just inside facing her was Louise.

She held out her arms and Narina ran to her.

"You have come. You have come!" called Louise. "Oh, Narina, I knew you would not fail me."

"It is *wonderful* to see you," enthused Narina, "and, of course, I came at once when you asked me to."

"I knew you would and I am very very grateful."

She kissed Narina and then she looked back at the Lord Chamberlain who was watching them.

"There were no difficulties?" she asked him.

He shook his head.

"Everything went according to your plan, ma'am, and I am quite certain that no one except ourselves, and of course, the coachman who I can trust, are aware that Miss Kenwin is now in the Palace."

Narina looked from one to the other in surprise.

"Why all this secrecy?" she asked nervously.

"I will tell you all about it," replied Louise.

"Then I will now leave you," murmured the Lord Chamberlain as he walked towards the door and only as he reached it, did he turn back to ask,

"Is there anything more you require, ma'am?"

Louise smiled at him.

"I am very sorry, I had quite forgotten, Narina, are you hungry or thirsty?" she enquired.

"I would love just a glass of lemonade, but I had something to eat before I left the Battleship."

"There is lemonade waiting in my sitting room, so goodnight, Lord Chamberlain, and thank you again for all your help."

The Lord Chamberlain bowed respectfully and left the room.

Louise then drew Narina into her sitting room.

It was a most attractive room and just as lovely as Narina had expected it would be and there were flowers everywhere and she thought that it was exactly the right background for Louise.

Louise fetched a glass of lemonade for her from the drinks table and then sat down on the sofa saying,

"I can see, dear Narina, that you are surprised and naturally curious to learn what is going on here."

"Yes, indeed, I am! Why was I only allowed to come ashore in the dark and why such secrecy in bringing me here?"

Louise gave a little laugh.

"It does sound rather strange, but I have asked you here because you are the only person in the world who can help me in our present predicament."

"You know that I am only too willing to help you, Louise, but you must tell me what I have to do and why."

"That is just what I would expect you would say, Narina. If you only knew how much I have missed you and how I long to share my troubles and difficulties with you."

Narina's eyes opened wider as she enquired

"It's not your husband, Prince Rudolf?"

"No, not the way you think of it. But in a way he is the reason why I need you so desperately."

Narina made herself more comfortable on the sofa.

"Tell me all about it from the beginning. It is too enigmatic so far for me to have the slightest idea what is going on."

"That is not surprising!"

Then Louise looked across the room as if to see that the door was firmly closed and almost instinctively Narina looked over her shoulder.

Then Louise began in a low voice,

"The situation here is extremely difficult, because we are being watched by the Russians night and day."

Narina drew in her breath.

She understood only too well, because she had so often discussed it with her Papa, how badly the Russians were behaving in the Balkans.

She was only too well aware that Queen Victoria had sent for Louise to marry a Balkan Prince and save his country from the Russian menace.

Now Narina asked Louise quickly,

"What are they doing? How can they harm Prince Rudolf now you are his wife?"

"That is the whole point, Narina, you know I have told you frequently in my letters how happy I am and what a wonderful husband Rudolf is to me."

"I have prayed that you would be happy, Louise."

"And I have prayed too when I came here. Rudolf fell in love with me and I with him the moment we met."

"Then what is wrong?" Narina demanded again.

"It is quite simple. We have been married for over two years and have not produced an heir to the throne."

Narina stared at her.

"But surely it is only a question of time – "

"That is what we thought at first, then we consulted one of our own doctors, who assured us there was nothing wrong with me, but that my husband needed a very small operation."

Narina was listening wide-eyed.

"Do you think that if he has it, you will – "

" – have children without any difficulty?" Louise finished.

"Then, of course, he must have it," Narina cried.

"That is exactly what we are going to do, but it is absolutely essential the Russians do not know about it."

"But why, Louise?"

"They have been closely watching Alexanderburg, hoping that our marriage would not last, in which case they would have every chance of taking over the country."

She felt Narina still did not understand and added,

"It is very easy out here for someone like Rudolf to have a fatal accident and then with no son to succeed him, the Russians would make an excuse to enter our territory, claiming that they came in to maintain order."

"Oh, now I am beginning to understand, Louise, so you desperately need a son."

"At least a dozen of them to be really safe and it is, as you know, something I long for. We always used to say when we were together how much we each hoped to have a large family so that they could never be lonely, as we were, being only children."

"Yes, of course," Narina agreed, "and that is what I was praying you would have."

"And that is what I was hoping too, but I can only do it with your help, Narina – "

Narina looked perplexed.

She could not see where she came in.

"What Rudolf and I are going to do, now you have arrived," Louise went on, "is to leave immediately while it is still dark for Constantinople."

Narina gave a cry of astonishment, but she did not interrupt and Louise continued,

"It would be a great mistake to have the operation here, where the Russians might bribe the doctor or in some way or another dispose of Rudolf when he was too weak to resist them."

"I cannot believe, Louise, that you have to live with anything so terrifying."

"Oh, we are used to it by now, but I am longing to have children and the operation, we are assured, is quite a minor one, but so essential if Alexanderburg is to survive."

"Then what do you want me to do?" asked Narina.

Louise smiled.

"I thought you would have guessed by now. We have always looked very much alike and, if you remember, we were called 'twins' when we were at school."

"You mean that *I* should to pretend to be *you*?"

"We shall not be away for more than two weeks at the most, but the greatest difficulty has been to think how we could travel to Constantinople without anyone knowing that Rudolf and I had left the Palace."

"And how are you going to do it?"

"The Lord Chamberlain is to announce tomorrow that Rudolf has had an accident out riding. As this has hurt his eyes, he now needs to stay in a dark room and rest."

She gave a deep sigh before adding,

"I am afraid, dearest Narina, it is going to be very difficult for you and I know you hate lying. But you will have to visit the empty bedroom two or three times a day, and tell everyone in the Palace that his eyes are improving and he will soon be back amongst them again."

"And they will have to believe that I am you?"

"That will not be too difficult, Narina. We really do look very like each other, and if you drive into the town you can always wear a large hat that will make it difficult for people to see your face clearly."

"What about the people in the Palace?"

"There is no reason for them to feel suspicious, as the few who will be in close contact with you are in on the secret."

"Who are they?"

"The Lord Chamberlain you will find to be a tower of strength, also Rudolf's personal servant, Paks, who will be the only one allowed to enter the sick room except for the doctor, an elderly man who is in on the secret and is officially the private physician to His Royal Highness.

"The maid who will look after you is a very dear person. Her name is Maria, and she has loved Rudolf ever since he was small. Only they will know that Rudolf and I have left. We will join the Battleship, which is waiting for us in a secluded harbour and return here the same way. I am sure we will manage it unnoticed."

"I do think it all very strange," murmured Narina.

Louise put out her hands to hold Narina's.

"There is no one else in the whole world who could do this for me, except you, my dearest Narina, and no one else would know how much it means to me."

"Of course I will do it for you, Louise. I am just so afraid I will let you down."

"I know you could never do that and I was thinking, as you were coming here, how well you acted in the school plays and they always gave you the leading part, because you were a far better actress than any of the rest of us!"

Narina could not deny this, but she merely smiled,

"I will do anything you ask of me, dearest Louise, but I am frightened in case I make a mess of it."

"You need not be worried about the language here as our language is a simple dialect of German, in which I know you are fluent. All you have to do is to be worried about your ailing husband and therefore you do not want to attend parties or give any in the Palace.

"In fact I am rather afraid, dearest Narina, that you may have to spend a lot of time on your own. But I know you enjoy reading and I promise that, when we return, you will have a riot of gaiety and meet all the most charming young men in the whole of Alexanderburg!"

Narina laughed.

"I am not worried about being alone or not meeting any men. As you know, there are very few I have found interesting at home. But I am afraid of making a mistake and that those who are not in on your secret may think that you are behaving very strangely."

"Just cling to the Lord Chamberlain, Narina, he has been wonderful ever since I arrived here. And as he adores Rudolf and thinks he is the best Ruler the country has ever had, he is so desperately afraid that the Russians will find some excuse to take us over."

"I can understand that must be prevented at all costs and I think your plan is a brilliant one."

"It is the only way Rudolf can have the operation without those Russians finding out all about it. They are so unscrupulous that I am certain, if they knew, they would find a way of hurting him – and even killing him."

Her voice shook and Narina put her arms round her.

"Don't worry, dearest. It is such a clever idea and I am sure that if we pray hard enough, the operation will be successful and he will be back on the throne before I can say 'Jack Robinson'."

Louise laughed.

"It will not be too difficult. Just smile at everyone and tell them they are all wonderful and then they will not bother you about anything else."

"I can only hope you are right, Louise," said Narina nervously. "Are you really leaving tonight?"

Louise jumped to her feet.

"I am now going to introduce you to my wonderful

and charming husband. He has been as worried as I have been in case you refused to come. When we received your letter saying that you would be joining us as quickly as the Battleship could bring you here, we both danced for joy."

She was talking as she walked across the room.

Now she opened a different door and called out,

"It's alright, Rudolf, come in and meet Narina."

Prince Rudolf entered the room and Narina saw at once why Louise fell in love with him.

He was tall with dark hair and extremely handsome.

She thought he looked so much like an Englishman and not in the least what she had expected of someone who lived in the Balkans.

As if she read Narina's thoughts, Louise explained,

"Rudolf's mother was English, and I have told him often that he could easily be taken for my brother."

Prince Rudolf smiled as he held out his hand,

"I am extremely grateful to you, Narina," he said in perfect English, "for coming to help us. As Louise has told you, *you* are the only person who can."

Narina, who had curtsied to him, replied,

"Of course I will always help Louise, but I am only so afraid, Your Royal Highness, of failing her."

"I am certain you will not. Having heard so much about you, I am sure you are as clever as, if not cleverer than my wife. And she is the brightest woman I have ever known!"

He smiled at Louise as he spoke and Narina could tell that he was very much in love with her.

"Now we must go," Louise announced in a brusque way. "I will put on my cape. Oh, and by the way, Narina, you must wear my clothes whilst you are here as everyone in the Palace will recognise them, and it will go a long way to making them think you are me."

"I shall look forward to it. I am sure that they are far smarter than anything I possess."

"I expect my wife has told you," Prince Rudolf said as Louise left the room, "that my valet, Paks, is not only in on our secret plan but you will find him a tower of strength in every way. He and I have been in some tight situations in the past and he has always made certain we came out of them unscathed."

"I hope he will look after me in the same way, but I cannot believe I will encounter any real danger."

He knew by the expression in her eyes that she was more than just a little scared.

"You are not to worry, Narina. I assure you that if you trust in Count Franz, the Lord Chamberlain, and Paks, you will be quite safe, and I hope happy, until we return."

Louise came hurrying back into the room.

"The Lord Chamberlain is waiting downstairs and we must get away now as quickly as possible."

"Of course," agreed Prince Rudolf.

Louise flung her arms round Narina.

"Thank you, thank you, dearest Narina, for being so fantastic. I knew you would not fail me and I only wish I could stay longer so that we could talk about old times."

"We can do that when you come back – "

"Yes indeed, and at the moment the most important thing is that Rudolf and I need no longer be afraid of those horrible menacing Russians."

"You really must not talk like that about the people we are trying to pretend are our friends," Prince Rudolf scolded her. "You must admit that I have been very astute so far in persuading them I really am quite fond of them."

"Rudolf is as good an actor as you are an actress, Narina, and we will prove it to you as soon as we return."

She kissed Narina again, hugging her as she did so.

Then as she turned to Prince Rudolf and curtsied, he bent and kissed her on the cheek.

"I am more grateful to you, Narina, than I can ever express in words. But I promise you one thing, Louise and I will find a beautiful present for you in Constantinople."

"All I really want is you both to come back safely and that I have acted your part well enough."

"I am sure that you will and I am quite prepared to take a bet on it," replied Prince Rudolf.

They were laughing as they went through the door.

As they did so, Narina saw the Lord Chamberlain waiting for them just outside.

Then as the door closed an elderly maid wearing a pretty lace-trimmed apron and a large cap to match on her grey hair entered the room through another door.

Narina smiled at her.

"I think you must be Maria."

"That's right, Lady," she replied in quite passable English. "Her Royal Highness has told me a lot about you and what a kind friend you are to her."

"That is what I hope I am and I do need your help, Maria. I am so afraid of making mistakes."

"None of us can make any mistakes for His Royal Highness's sake, and a finer and kinder Prince no country's ever had."

She turned back through the door, saying,

"Come and see, Lady, where you will be sleeping and I'll show you His Royal Highness's room."

They were two huge rooms and Narina could only think that they were breathtakingly beautiful.

The Prince's room which for centuries every Ruler of Alexanderburg had occupied was much further along the passage and its windows looked out over the gardens.

The bed was the most impressive Narina had ever seen. It was draped in crimson velvet and everything else about it appeared to be of solid gold.

The bed-head was beautifully carved with flowers and birds and directly above the front of the canopy there were three golden cupids holding up a star.

Narina was told later that the star was the emblem of Alexanderburg and it appeared on everything connected with the Royal family.

Opening out of the Prince's bedroom was another room as tastefully decorated as any room Narina had ever seen. It was all in a soft blue and there was an abundance of flowers arranged everywhere.

Narina knew at once that Louise must have ordered them for her because she knew how much she loved them.

"It's the prettiest room ever!" she exclaimed.

Maria obviously took her remark as a compliment.

"I thinks as how you'd say that, Lady. As you'll understand, Her Royal Highness always sleeps next door and that's where it'll be wise for you to sleep even though you use this room to dress in."

Narina understood and then she asked,

"Are you certain that no one in the Palace except the Lord Chamberlain, you and His Royal Highness's valet will be aware that they have left for Constantinople?"

"I do hears all the gossip, Lady, and they're just so sorry that His Royal Highness has hurt his eyes. They'd never guess he was slipping off with Her Royal Highness."

"Then I can see we must be very careful, Maria, I think it would be wise if you hid my luggage which I see they have brought up here."

She had noticed her case when she had come into the bedroom and Maria then moved it to a large wardrobe which stood at the far end of the room.

Narina hurried to help her.

"Now don't you worry, Lady."

"But it is heavy," protested Narina, "because I put in so much I thought I would need, including some books."

"There'll be plenty of books here in the Palace and Her Royal Highness has left a few she thinks you'd like in the sitting room."

Narina thought it was just like Louise to remember her passion for books and to find some she would enjoy.

As she had been told, she would doubtless have to spend long hours alone in the sitting room and if she was pretending to the world outside she was with her injured husband, she would certainly need plenty of books.

"Now what you must do, Lady," Maria piped up, "is to retire to bed early and have a really good night's rest. Everything'll seem far better in the morning."

Narina laughed as Maria was talking to her just like her old nanny, who always believed that 'a good night's sleep' would solve any number of problems.

Maria helped her undress and when she had shown her Prince Rudolf's bedroom, Narina commented,

"I would far rather sleep here in this smaller room with the flowers. If anyone is aware of it, although I see no reason why they should be, you can always tell them I was afraid I might keep my husband awake and thus his injuries would not heal so quickly."

Maria smiled benignly.

"You do as you would wish, Lady, and this room's as pretty as you."

"Thank you, Maria, but what I would want you to say is that I am as pretty as Her Royal Highness. Do you think anyone will notice the difference between us?"

"I'll make your hair just like Her Royal Highness," offered Maria, "and you will see very few people as your husband is ill."

"I quite understand, but you must tell me, Maria, all you can about anyone who does come to see me, so that I do not make any silly mistakes."

"I do that," Maria promised, "and as the sun is very bright we'll pull them sunshades over the windows when people come to see you."

Narina thought that this was good thinking.

She climbed into the pretty blue bed which boasted an exceedingly comfortable mattress.

Maria put a glass of water by her bed and blew out all the candles except for two burning beside the bed.

She made a quick bob and murmured in her own language,

"Goodnight, Your Royal Highness. God grant you sleep well."

Before Narina could think of a suitable reply, she had left the room closing the door behind her.

She blew out the candles by her bed and now the room was in darkness except for a faint shimmer of light that came from the moon riding high in the clear sky.

The same moon would be shining down on the ship carrying Louise and Prince Rudolf, as they would steam from the Black Sea down the Bosporus to Constantinople.

It would not take them too long and by the morning His Royal Highness would be in the hospital awaiting his operation.

Narina could well understand how important it was

to him and Louise and equally important to keep what they were doing a secret from the enemy.

Then as she lay back against the plush pillows, she asked herself again how this could all be happening to her.

Never for a moment had she imagined anything so fantastic when she was living quietly with her father in St. Albans.

Now she suddenly found herself in the middle of a Balkan intrigue against the might of the Russian Empire.

And how was it going to be possible for her to keep up her disguise as the wife of the reigning Prince?

'This cannot be true', Narina almost cried out. 'It must be a dream.'

Then she told herself it was all a story to amuse and delight her Papa.

Perhaps when she was older, she would write the whole saga down in a book and it would become a tale of high adventure for her children and her grandchildren.

As she and Louise had always done things together, she was sure this was something Louise would do too.

They could compete with each other as to who was the better authoress and which of them could produce the most dramatic and exciting account of this exploit.

It all sounded so funny that Narina laughed aloud.

She was still laughing silently to herself as finally she fell asleep.

*

When she woke up in the morning, it was because Maria was pulling back the curtains.

"I hopes Your Royal Highness slept well – "

For a moment Narina thought she was addressing her by mistake and then she remembered what she had said the previous evening.

"Very well thank you so much, Maria, I think I was tired after so much excitement last night."

"Everyone downstairs in the Palace hopes that His Royal Highness had a good night and they ask Paks."

Narina recalled that Paks was Prince Rudolf's valet and that she would be wise to meet him.

She now realised that Maria was waiting for her to get out of bed and she found her bath was ready for her in front of the fireplace.

Narina had been so fast asleep she had not heard it being brought in and she learnt later that it was not only by Maria, who could not have managed it alone, but with the help of Paks.

There was hot and cold water in polished brass cans just like the ones in use in England.

Her bath was scented with flowers which she could not recognise, but she thought that she should be able to identify them before she left Alexanderburg.

Then Maria helped her dress and she put on a very pretty day gown that she was told had come from Paris and Her Royal Highness had purchased it on her last visit.

Narina then sat down at the dressing table on which there was a mirror framed with carved golden cupids.

Maria arranged her hair in a very different style.

It was the way Louise wore hers and Narina felt it was most becoming and it made her look a little older.

The style was so much like Louise's that when she looked in the mirror, she found it hard to recognise herself.

Maria insisted that she apply a little powder on her nose and a touch of lip salve on her lips.

"I have never used make-up before," said Narina.

"Your Royal Highness should move with the times.

Everyone so smart in Alexanderburg. They copy Viennese and the Viennese copy the French."

Narina laughed.

"So that's what it amounts to."

"Lady look very pretty – and *very* Royal."

Narna now giggled and looked again in the mirror.

She had to admit she did look quite different from a Bishop's daughter.

Breakfast was served in her sitting room and for the first time she met Paks.

He was a man of nearly forty and Narina felt that no one seeing the twinkle in his eyes and his rather strange and unusual face would connect him with such an adventure and perhaps drama.

He bowed to her politely as she entered the room and he addressed her as Maria had done.

When she had finished breakfast, he suggested,

"If Your Royal Highness should wish to go into the garden, please inform me and I'll make sure that there's no one watching who we don't trust."

"You don't think there is likely to be anyone hostile or foreign in the garden?" asked Narina.

Paks made an expressive movement with his hands.

"One just never knows. In these days, Your Royal Highness, even the walls have ears. We has to be careful, very very careful, for His Royal Highness be our lifeline to happiness."

The way he spoke to her with a strong accent made the words seem as unreal as everything else did to Narina.

She could hardly believe it was possible for her to be treated like a Princess and to be moving about in these beautiful rooms.

Now she was aware that they held a great number of treasures which she must inspect when she had the time.

As her breakfast was carried away, Paks came back to announce,

"His Royal Highness's Lord Chamberlain requests an audience with Your Royal Highness."

"Please ask him to come in."

The Lord Chamberlain bowed deeply to her in the Royal manner and as Paks left the room, he came towards where Narina was sitting on the sofa.

"Are you all right?" he enquired.

"I am feeling that I am sitting in the clouds," Narina answered, "and that this cannot be happening to me. At the same time it is all very exciting."

The Lord Chamberlain laughed and as he remained standing, Narina suggested,

"Please sit down, Lord Chamberlain."

"I was waiting for you to invite me to do so."

Narina gave a little gasp.

"Am I to play my part even when we are alone?"

"To be a good actor or actress, you have to act not only with your body but also with your mind. So you must think you are what you pretend to be, otherwise it might be easy for someone to discover that you are acting a part."

Narina smiled.

"I understand, so please tell me more of what I have to do and I promise to try to be perfect in my part so that you never have to rebuke me."

The Lord Chamberlain sat down.

"I am rather afraid, Your Royal Highness, that this afternoon you have to receive a group of women who come here every year as guests of the Mayor."

"But I thought I just had to stay here reading a book until Louise and His Royal Highness return."

"That is what we hoped you would be able to do, but unfortunately this appointment was made by one of my *aides-de-camp* who forgot to tell me about it. It is too late to cancel it now, as they will have already left their homes in the country and will be travelling for the City."

Narina drew in her breath.

"Suppose I make a mistake?"

"I am quite sure you have often attended exactly the same type of occasion with your father."

"Well if you put it like that, I have," she admitted.

"Then you know what to do and it really consists of listening, being sympathetic to their grievances, if any, and as far as you are concerned, doing nothing. I am told that you are fluent in German, so language will be no problem."

"You are quite certain, Lord Chamberlain, that they will not realise that I am not who I pretend to be."

"Why should they? Most of the ladies come from outside the City and have never seen you before. All you have to do is to behave as you would at home to people in your father's flock who are on an outing."

It was impossible for Narina not to laugh at what he was saying, because it was so true.

He bowed once again and left her.

Narina went to her room and stood at the window looking out towards the sea.

She was thinking how bizarre it all was.

In a twinkling of an eye she had been transmitted from her quiet home in Hertfordshire to this strange land, where the local people were striving against being overrun by their greedy and aggressive neighbour.

'They are small,' she mused, 'and very vulnerable. Is it really possible that the Union Jack in the shape of the wife of the ruling Prince can possibly save them?'

Then it was as if the answer to her question came to her straight from Heaven.

She realised that whatever the cost, Louise, and all those who were so proud of being British would stand and fight – they would defy the enemy and never give in.

Looking up at the sky as the sunshine was turning the garden into a fairyland of intense beauty, Narina prayed that she would play her part, however small, perfectly and without fault –

That God would give her the strength and resilience that Alexanderburg so desperately needed.

CHAPTER THREE

Dressed in one of Louise's gowns and wearing one of her prettiest hats over her newly arranged hair, Narina walked slowly downstairs.

There she found an equerry waiting to escort her to the City Hall where the women were congregating.

The equerry was a young and rather good-looking man and he was obviously impressed by Princess Louise as he took Narina to be.

He sat in the seat of the carriage opposite to her and Narina thought he looked at her nervously.

"You must tell me all about the people who I will be meeting," she asked, "and where they have come from. I forgot to ask the Lord Chamberlain to give me a list."

"I have brought it with me just in case Your Royal Highness wanted it."

"How clever of you! And you must remind me of the different places I have visited, just in case they mention somewhere where I have been, as they will be annoyed if I don't remember it."

The equerry laughed.

"It is rather difficult when there are so many small towns and villages in Alexanderburg. Also as I come from Vienna, I find it hard to remember the different names."

"Then I just hope they will not notice how ignorant we both are!"

She realised she had put the equerry at his ease and then she found herself immensely interested in the City.

She saw it was very pleasantly laid out and the trees bordering the streets gave it a most attractive appearance.

They passed by the Cathedral and Narina was just about to say she wished to visit it when she remembered that Louise would have been married there – and doubtless she had been there for other occasions such as Easter Day.

'I must be so careful not to forget I am not myself,' she reminded herself.

The City Hall was a very impressive building.

She was met by the Lord Mayor in full regalia and several Councillors and the women curtsied low while the men bowed over her hand.

Then she was taken to a huge hall that was literally packed with women.

The Lord Mayor made a long speech saying how grateful they all were to Princess Louise for attending their annual meeting.

From what he said, Narina gathered that this was the Alexanderburg equivalent of the Mothers' Union.

When the Lord Mayor finished speaking, he turned to Narina and enquired,

"I wonder, Your Royal Highness, if you would like to say a few words to the assembled ladies."

"Of course I would," replied Narina.

She was thankful as she rose to her feet that she had practised so much of the Alexanderburg language with the Baron on the Battleship.

She knew that she was almost word perfect.

Remembering that she was supposed to be Louise, she spoke of her happy childhood in England and how she had attended an English School.

"I know," she insisted, "that His Royal Highness, my husband, is very anxious to improve our facilities for education here in Alexanderburg.

"But what you must do and this is very important, is to make your children interested in learning even before they go to school."

She told them about some of the lessons her father had taught her and how it was essential for young children to learn to read as early as possible.

"I have always been so grateful that I can read book after book and find every single one entrancing. That is an education in itself and every child should begin by reading a simple fairy tale."

She realised that the women were listening intently as she continued,

"I am sure that you will have lots of questions you would like to ask. Perhaps no one has the time in this busy country to answer you. Therefore do please ask me now and I will try to answer as best as I can."

She saw that the Lord Mayor and the Councillors with him were astonished.

One woman asked Narina which fairy story she felt was best for children and another asked if it was a mistake for children to love their toys more than their parents.

Narina smiled at these questions.

"I think the truth is that a child wants a companion and if they do not have another child to play with they will begin to believe that their dolls and teddy bears are living persons – someone they can talk to and who will answer them in their own language.

"My advice to you is simple. If you want a child to be happy and if you can give it a new playmate by having another child as near its age as possible, then do so."

There was laughter at this advice and she could see that the women were interested.

And so the questions came thick and fast.

Then as the majority of the women in the hall had their children with them, Narina announced,

"Now I am coming down from the platform and I would like to see your children. I do think they have been very good whilst I have been speaking and that you have brought them all up exceedingly well."

The women were delighted.

As she started to walk round, one of the babies who was very young and in its mother's arms, started to cry.

The woman rocked the baby, rose from her seat and walked about with it, but still the baby cried.

It was then that Narina remembered something her mother had done once.

A child had cried at a meeting when her father was speaking and he was always irritated if he was interrupted and her mother took great pains to keep the children happy.

Narina turned to a Councillor standing beside her.

"Can you fetch me some honey?" she asked.

"Honey!" he exclaimed.

"Yes please, honey and a teaspoon."

He sent a servant off to find the honey.

In a few moments the servant came hurrying back with a comb of honey on a plate and a small teaspoon.

Narina scooped up some of the honey that had run out of the comb and put it gently on the baby's lips.

For a while he went on crying and then as he tasted the honey, he began to enjoy it.

He sucked away at what was already on his tongue until Narina placed more honey in his mouth.

"Now he will go to sleep," she told his mother.

"I never thinks," replied the woman, "of giving the baby honey."

"Honey is quite wonderful for children. My mother always gave it to me when I was small. It is very useful if you are travelling and small children are upset by bumping over rough roads and therefore they cry."

There was a murmur of appreciation in the hall.

"Give them honey. I promise you, if they wake up in the night and it annoys your husband, give them a little honey to suck and they will soon go to sleep again. And if you are lucky they will not wake up until the morning."

There was another murmur of interest.

Just as she completed her tour around the room, the Lord Mayor announced that tea was served and although it was a tight squeeze, he felt sure that everyone would find enough for themselves and their children to eat.

He took Narina into his private apartment where tea was served for her and the Councillors.

"I am very certain, Your Royal Highness," the Lord Mayor said, "that all these women will have something to talk about until next year."

Narina laughed.

"It always surprises me that people in the country, although they do keep bees, are not aware of the wonderful properties of honey. They make jam, which is not half as good for them as honey. Mohammed once said, '*Honey is the food of the body and the soul*'."

She spoke as she would have spoken to her father and then she saw surprise in the Lord Mayor's eyes.

Only then did she remember that Louise, much as she loved her, was not as well read as she was.

Tactfully she changed the subject to ask what was happening in the City.

There was a moment's hesitation before the Lord Mayor replied,

"Everything is pretty quiet, Your Royal Highness, but I have a suspicion that there are intruders from outside who join the men in the evening when work is done. From all I hear they are trying to unsettle them in various subtle ways that is impossible for us to control."

"Then what is the answer?" enquired Narina.

"I think that what Your Royal Highness has done this afternoon has been of great help. The women are very delighted with you. It will give them much to talk about, and they will not be so attentive to their husbands tonight."

"Are you suggesting, Lord Mayor, that the people are being made to feel misgoverned and oppressed?"

"Only in certain districts at the moment, but we are always afraid that the situation might grow worse as it has in other Balkan countries."

"What I feel is important," asserted Narina, "is that they should see much more of my husband and me in the future. I had the feeling when I was talking to the women just now that either most of them were newcomers to the country or else I had missed them on past occasions when I have appeared in public."

"You were unable to grace this meeting last year. And also the previous year, which was just after you were married, as you were away on your honeymoon."

"That, naturally, was a good excuse for not being present, but before I leave I would like once again to talk to the women who are having tea in the other room."

The Lord Mayor was obviously surprised.

"I think we are asking too much of you, Your Royal Highness."

"Not at all. I talked, as you saw, to a great number of them, but I did not reach them all and some may feel neglected."

Despite the Lord Mayor's rather feeble protest, she insisted on doing as she wished.

She walked into where the women were finishing their tea and some of them were already putting coats on their small children.

Before the Lord Mayor was aware of what she was intending to do, Narina stood up on one of the chairs.

The women looked up in anticipation as she raised her voice and began,

"I have come back not only to say goodbye to you but because I have an idea that I think you will all enjoy. In two months time, when the weather will be warmer, will you try to come back again? But before you do so will you please send in a drawing or a toy that your children have made themselves.

"There will be a good number of prizes, including for the funniest exhibit and the most imaginative as well as for those which are outstandingly clever."

"I am sure that the Lord Mayor will give us a date before you leave and the exhibition will, I am quite certain, be of considerable interest to the many tourists who will be visiting Alexanderburg in July and August."

There was a distinct gasp of excitement and then all the women started to clap and cheer.

Narina's idea had very obviously appealed to their imagination and they were thrilled at the idea of showing how clever their children were.

Helped by the Lord Mayor, she slipped down from the chair and then she started talking to them individually.

"That be something so new, Your Royal Highness,"

one woman said, "and as I've five children, they'll all be hoping they can win a prize."

"I hope they will too, and I promise you there will be plenty of prizes. In fact my husband and I will work out exactly how many different ways they can compete so that no one is left out."

She shook hands with one mother after another.

When finally she left long after the Lord Mayor had expected her to do so, they all cheered her, not only in the City Hall but outside as she stepped into her carriage.

Then they waved until she was out of sight.

When she was alone with the equerry, he said,

"If you will excuse me, Your Royal Highness, that was an absolutely brilliant idea of yours. I have often felt that the women are neglected and forgotten."

"I think if nothing else it will give them something new to talk about," added Narina.

"And I am certain there will be a big rush for honey after all Your Royal Highness has said. Actually the honey in this country is exceptionally good."

"I look forward to enjoying it myself."

She realised that she had spoken as if she had not tasted Alexanderburg honey before.

Quickly, to cover up what she knew was a definite *faux pas*, she added,

"I think in the Palace the cooks believe that honey is too simple and do not provide it as much as I would like. They prefer to send it up for only breakfast."

She was speaking as her mother might have spoken.

Then she thought that perhaps the women she had just left might think it rather strange that while she was so interested in children, she still had none of her own.

Almost instinctively she found herself praying that Prince Rudolf's trip to Constantinople would be successful and that there would soon be an heir to the throne.

As they neared the Palace, the equerry piped up,

"Would it be forward of me, Your Royal Highness, to say how much I have admired you this afternoon? And how impressed I was with the way you handled not only the women but also the Lord Mayor?"

Narina gave a little laugh.

"Did I handle him?" she quizzed.

"Your Royal Highness did indeed. He is so much a stickler for everything being done exactly as it has always been done before. I saw his surprise when you insisted on going into the ladies' tea room."

"I can see that he is rather a fuddy-duddy. We shall have to teach him that the Palace requires everything to be new and exciting for those we reign over."

"Your Royal Highness has certainly struck the first blow this afternoon and the City will be talking of nothing else before they go to bed.

Narina was also praised when she arrived back at the Palace by the Lord Chamberlain.

He had been told what had happened and came up to the sitting room where she was reading.

"I hear that you burst a bombshell under the Lord Mayor this afternoon, Your Royal Highness!"

"I hope I did not do anything wrong – "

"No, you were completely and absolutely right. It is something we should have thought of before and I blame myself for not doing so."

He was smiling as he shook his head and went on,

"To be honest, I have forgotten how important the

women are. But you have brilliantly created a new defence against the Russians that has not entered our minds."

"If in a small way," Narina answered him, "I have forged a new weapon against them, I shall be very proud."

"You have every right to be. I was so stupid not to realise that women have a tremendous influence over their husbands. Every husband when he goes to bed tonight will have to listen not only to how charming you are, but how you have given an important incentive to their children."

"I am very glad that you are not angry with me for interfering, but it seemed sad for those women, who had come long distances just to have a brief glance at who they thought was their Princess, and go home with nothing else to talk about."

"You were absolutely right," the Lord Chamberlain replied. "And now they will talk incessantly for the next two months about their children and the prizes they hope they will win."

"There must be lots of prizes. It would be a good idea if every child took something away, even if it was not a first or second prize, when they leave the City Hall."

"It is certainly a great idea – "

"Perhaps it could be a tiny book or for the smaller children a little doll. I am sure it must be possible to give a prize to those who are really outstanding, and at the same time to give the others something to take home with them."

"I have always heard," said the Lord Chamberlain, "that your father is an exceedingly clever man and I now realise that you have followed in his footsteps."

"I like to think I have in a small way. It is terribly sad that Papa did not have a son. It is what he would have loved above all else. But it has meant that I have spent a great deal more time with him than I would have done if I had not been an only child."

"The one thing I am quite certain about is that we are extremely fortunate to have you here and if you go on springing surprises on us as you have today, I think that Their Royal Highnesses when they return here will be most grateful to you."

"I am praying very hard that their secret departure will give them what they really want."

"An heir to the throne will give us the security we do not have at the moment, but in the meantime you have erected a new wall of defence that I and all my colleagues are extremely grateful for."

*

When she climbed into bed that night, Narina found herself thinking over what the Lord Chamberlain had said.

She reflected that it was a bit of good luck that she should have to take Louise's place because the date of the meeting had been overlooked.

'There must be other ways,' she thought to herself, 'to make it more difficult for the Russians to intervene.'

But for the moment her mind was blank.

However, she felt certain that she would be guided as she had been this afternoon into saying the right words at the right moment.

She longed to tell her father all that had happened.

She was sure that when she did, he would believe it was due to his prayers and hers that she had been guided in how to help Louise on her first day of impersonating her.

Because she was supposed to be with her husband, Narina had eaten dinner alone in her sitting room.

The food was brought upstairs by footmen and Paks and Maria took it from them in the doorway.

The Palace chefs naturally sent up dinner and every other meal for two people and as the plates had to go back empty, both Maria and Paks protested they were putting on weight!

"What we don't eat, Your Royal Highness, we then gives to the birds in the garden," Paks told her. "There's double the number waiting there now. It's an ill wind that blows no one any good!"

Narina laughed, but she had to admit the food was delicious and she herself was eating more than she would have done ordinarily.

"Are the Palace staff very curious about His Royal Highness's illness?" she asked Maria.

"Paks has told them that his eyes be getting better, but the doctors insist his room's kept dark and no sunshine allowed in for fear it strains his sight.

"Paks also tells them that His Royal Highness hurt his head when he fell and he therefore has to be kept as quiet as possible."

Narina was aware that Paks and Maria had made it impossible for anyone to guess there was actually no one in the Royal bedroom.

She knew that Paks locked the door at night and it was widely reported that the doctor had said that His Royal Highness must not be disturbed by any noise.

None of the housemaids were allowed into the three private rooms where Narina spent her time.

*

The next day Narina realised she had nothing to do.

Therefore she took one of the books her father had given her out of her trunk and after locking it again, she put the key into her handbag where no one would find it.

Then she told Maria she was going into the private garden to sit in the sunshine.

"You'll be safe there, Your Royal Highness, and no one'll interrupt you as His Royal Highness decreed some time ago that he and his wife must have somewhere they could sunbathe and not be seen by prying eyes."

"That was indeed sensible of him."

"Well, you'll find the garden nice and quiet and no one'll come near you, but don't you go sitting in the sun without a hat or a sunshade. It's red hot in the afternoon."

"Yes, I realise that, but as I seldom wear a hat I will sit under the trees in the shade."

"Now you wait until I gives a order to the gardener to put a comfortable seat with a cushion under the trees and make sure no one intrudes for the rest of the afternoon."

Narina thanked her, but did not make any comment.

She had thought it would be interesting to talk to one of the gardeners about the flowers of Alexanderburg.

Equally as Louise had been here for over two years, she should know the answer by this time and it would seem stupid to make the gardener surprised at her ignorance.

She thought that it would have been much more fun if Louise was here with her at this moment and they could laugh about everything that had happened –

'I will talk to her when she returns,' she decided.

Then suddenly something struck her which she had not thought of before.

If she remained after Louise returned, it would be a great mistake for the two of them to be seen together.

There would doubtless be speculation about their looking so alike and people would wonder whether at one time or another they had been deceived into thinking that Princess Louise was actually the girl from England.

'That means,' Narina reflected, 'I will have to leave as soon as they arrive home.'

It certainly seemed as if it would be impossible for her to stay on and she could only think despairingly, if that was right, that she would never have a moment alone with Louise as she longed for.

'Maybe I could go away from here and then come back again,' she pondered.

But she was not certain that it would be as easy as it sounded.

'Anyway it's just no use me getting worked up now whether or not I will have to leave. There is undoubtedly much for me to do as 'Princess Louise' before I leave.'

She found that the small narrow staircase which she had been unable to see in the darkness when she arrived had a very pretty carpet.

There were watercolour paintings of the garden on the walls and she wondered who could have painted them.

Then she thought perhaps she would have a chance to talk about them to the Lord Chamberlain.

She knew that he had a good sense of humour and she felt it would be interesting if they could ever be alone together for an hour or so.

As Narina reached the private garden, she then told herself that she really had no need for other people.

The beauty of the flowers and the attractive way the garden itself was designed was a delight she would have loved to show her father.

There were walls covered with bright clematis and there was a fountain playing in the middle of the lawn.

And a small cascade flowed through the trees rising behind the Palace and continued through the garden before disappearing from sight.

The comfortable seat which had been arranged for her was in the shade of trees still in blossom.

Narina found that when she sat down, she could not be seen from the windows of the Palace.

Indeed she was now sitting in an enchanted world of beauty that could only have sprung from the imagination of a lover of flowers.

Because it was so beautiful and there was the soft tinkle of the cascade, Narina did not at once open her book.

She sat enraptured, looking around her.

Hearing the birds in the trees, the hum of the bees and seeing the butterflies moving in and out of the lilies.

It was all so lovely, she felt it could not be real.

Equally she could not help but wish that her father or someone special was enjoying all this beauty with her.

'If Louise was here,' she now mused to herself, 'we would have so much to say. And if Papa was here, I know that he would be able to tell me a thousand things about all these flowers, the trees and even the sky.'

Then she laughed at herself.

She was finding fault and should not dare to do that in a place which must be a part of Paradise.

'It is all so glorious. How could there possibly be anything ugly or unpleasant in a place with such beauty?'

She knew from the manner in which Louise and her husband had stolen so surreptitiously away from the Palace that danger threatened Alexanderburg.

It was real and not part of anyone's imagination.

"This incredible beauty must never be spoilt," she found herself exclaiming aloud.

Then resolutely she opened the book her father had given her.

As she might have guessed, it was exactly the sort of book she would enjoy in such a place.

It told her stories and legends of the Balkans and of Saints and past heroes who had left their imprint upon the people and the country.

'It is so like my Papa to guess what I would want to read at this particular moment,' pondered Narina.

Yet it was difficult to read when everything around her was so lovely to look at.

She was afraid that, if she took her eyes off it, the garden might disappear.

Two white doves appeared suddenly in the sky.

Then they both fluttered down on the lawn near the fountain, which in itself, she felt, could tell a story if only it could speak.

The carved stone bowl was obviously very old and she had noticed as she passed that there were water lilies in it and a flash of gold told her there were also goldfish.

The water flung up by the fountain into the sky was like a shimmering rainbow until it cascaded downwards in an embracing circle.

It was so beautiful and unusual that Narina was sure there must be a story attached to the fountain in the book her father had given her.

Once again she could not suppress the feeling that she would really like to share her thoughts and ideas with someone else.

'Am I just asking too much when I have you,' she murmured looking down at the lilies beside her and then at the trees rising high on the other side of the garden.

Resolutely she opened her book again.

Even as she did so, she noticed a number of birds were suddenly flying out of the trees above her and across the garden.

She wondered what had disturbed them.

She thought it was perhaps some large animal since no human being could possibly be there.

Then she was suddenly aware of heavy footsteps.

Someone was running through the trees!

Even as she stared, feeling as if it could not be true, a man appeared in front of her.

One glance at him made her draw in her breath.

A second glance made her rise to her feet.

He was a tall man with broad shoulders and there was blood on the shirt he was wearing which was torn as if he had been roughly used.

There was blood on his forehead and on one cheek.

She stared at him.

Then he called out in a deep but breathless voice,

"Princess Louise, I am English and the Russians are just behind me!"

CHAPTER FOUR

As the man finished speaking, Narina knew at once what she must do.

"Follow me!" she called out and started to run.

As quickly as she could, she ran over the lawn, past the fountain and up to the Palace.

The door to the private staircase was in front of her and she could hear as she reached it that the man was just behind her.

She rushed in and almost as if she had told him to, he locked the door behind them.

Still without speaking, she ran up the stairs and he followed her.

She paused for a second before she stepped into the corridor where Prince Rudolf's bedroom was situated.

There was just a chance that one of the housemaids might be working at the end of the corridor, but to her great relief there was no one there.

Even as she stepped out followed by the man, Paks appeared.

Breathless because she had been running so quickly her voice came jerkily from between her lips.

"Paks please – this man with me is English – and the Russians are just behind him. Hide him in His Royal Highness's bed as he will be safe there."

Paks, as she might have expected, took one look at the man who had followed her and muttered,

"Come this way, sir."

He opened the door of Prince Rudolf's room and as he slipped into it, Paks suggested,

"Your Royal Highness should now inform the Lord Chamberlain of what has happened."

Narina nodded.

It was what she intended to do anyway.

For a second she was too overwhelmed to say or do anything.

She stood drawing in her breath and then slowly she walked down the corridor to the main staircase.

As she anticipated there were a number of servants in the hall below as well as two *aides-de-camp*.

She deliberately forced herself to walk downstairs slowly.

When she reached the bottom, one of the *aides-de-camp* hurried to her side.

"Is there anything I can do, Your Royal Highness?" he enquired.

"I wish to speak to the Lord Chamberlain," Narina replied. "And if he is busy, tell him it is very urgent."

"Yes, of course, Your Royal Highness. If you will come this way, I will take you now to his Office."

The *aide-de-camp* walked on and she followed him.

Narina deliberately did not look round in case she might be delayed by people wanting to speak to her.

She had been aware, although she had not thought about it until now, that Louise had been sensible enough to send her Ladies-in-Waiting away on holiday.

Louise had told them she would be going nowhere and doing nothing except look after her husband and they had best enjoy themselves while they had the opportunity.

Narina thought now it would be very difficult if she had endless Ladies-in-Waiting in attendance as they would have expected to be with her wherever she appeared.

After walking to the far end of the Palace, the *aide-de-camp* stopped at a waiting room.

It had several rather uncomfortable chairs arranged stiffly round a table in the middle of the room and Narina thought there was nothing to recommend it.

"If Your Royal Highness would wait here for just a moment," suggested the *aide-de-camp*, "I will go and see if the Lord Chamberlain is free and tell him that Your Royal Highness wishes to see him."

"Thank you – very much," Narina managed to say.

She knew that it was imagination, but she was still feeling breathless both from running so fast and from being overcome by the sudden appearance of the Englishman.

He had said the Russians were just behind him, but she had no idea how many.

There might be just a few or perhaps even as many as an Army could now be infiltrating Alexanderburg before anyone was aware of it.

The *aide-de-camp* was away for just a few minutes and he smiled as he returned.

"The Lord Chamberlain's visitor has just left," he said as if it was an achievement in itself, "and now he is waiting for Your Royal Highness."

She followed the *aide-de-camp* and he opened the door of the adjoining room.

She could see at a glance that the room was very different from the one she had just left.

The bright sun was streaming in through two large windows opening onto the garden and the walls were hung with magnificent pictures.

At any other time she would have stayed to admire them.

As it was, she could only hurry across the room to where the Lord Chamberlain was waiting for her.

As she heard the door closing behind her and knew that they were alone, she said in almost a whisper,

"There are Russians – approaching us! I have just taken a wounded Englishman they were chasing – up into Prince Rudolf's bedroom."

The Lord Chamberlain stared at her in amazement.

As he saw how pale she was and how agitated from the way she spoke, he proposed quietly,

"Sit down and tell me what has happened. I can see it has upset you."

"I am terrified for all of you, but it might be only a few Russians who were chasing him. I did not actually see anyone."

"Start from the beginning and tell me exactly what has happened."

"I went into the garden to read, having nothing else – to do," Narina began.

Despite herself she was visibly trembling and her voice was even more jerky than it had been before.

The Lord Chamberlain did not speak, but rose and walked to a side table holding a number of decanters.

Narina saw him pour a liquid into a glass and then he brought it back and put it in her hand.

"Drink this slowly," he advised her. "Then please go on with what you were telling me."

She sipped it and realised it was a local brandy and she had been given some before by Maria.

"It's sweet and it's made from our local grapes," she had said proudly. "And I finds it delicious."

Narina sipped the liquid slowly and then when she felt that her heart was no longer banging inside her body, she continued,

"I am sorry to seem so stupid, but having seen this man I knew you would want – to know there are Russians near us."

"I will come and talk to the man you have rescued, but first go on with your story. You have not yet told me exactly what has happened."

In a calm voice and now speaking almost normally, Narina related how she had heard the man coming through the trees behind her.

"When he said, *'the Russians are just behind me,'* I knew there was no time to lose."

The Lord Chamberlain smiled.

"I might well have guessed you would be sensible and as your father's daughter, extremely resourceful."

He paused before he added,

"Any other woman would have questioned him. In which case the Russians might have appeared and carried him and *you* away."

Narina gave a cry,

"That was just what I was afraid might happen."

"Naturally you were. Now I will come and talk to this Englishman and find out who he is and why he is in trouble with the Russians."

"Do you not think that a whole Army of Russians is approaching us at this moment?"

The Lord Chamberlain shook his head.

"If there was a whole Army of them, our guards on the frontier would have notified us by this time. I think, although I may be mistaken, this is a one man battle."

Narina looked relieved.

"I hope you are right, Lord Chamberlain."

"I am hoping the same myself."

He saw that Narina had emptied her glass and took it from her.

"Now we will walk slowly back as if we are only concerned about His Royal Highness's eyesight and then we will find out exactly who you have rescued."

"I never thought anything like this could happen so near to the Palace," Narina remarked nervously.

"Where those rapacious Russians are concerned, it might be anywhere," the Lord Chamberlain replied.

In a more concerned tone he added,

"Are you sure that you feel like walking back? We can rest a little longer if you wish to."

"No, of course not, anything may be happening and you may have to send out soldiers to capture the Russians who are obviously trying to take this man a prisoner."

"We will soon find out the truth."

The Lord Chamberlain opened the door of the room and they walked back the way Narina had come.

He stopped to greet several visitors whom he had not yet seen and told them he would be with them as soon as he was free, but he did not introduce them to Narina.

The *aides-de-camp* in the hall waited for his orders, but he did not give any.

They walked slowly up the stairs and only as they reached the top did Narina glance back and see the *aides-de-camp* talking with each other.

She guessed they were speculating as to why she had called for the Lord Chamberlain – they were obviously thinking that perhaps His Royal Highness had taken a turn for the worse.

However, she did not say anything.

They walked in silence down the long corridors to the Royal apartments.

Only as they reached them did Narina say,

"Can I come in with you, or shall I wait outside?"

He considered for a moment and then he smiled,

"As you are responsible for this man and for putting him where he is, I think I would be very ungracious if I left you in ignorance."

Narina felt relieved as she had been thinking that it would be frustrating and ignominious to be left outside, as after all the stranger had been clearly fighting the Russians and was injured while doing so.

He knocked on the door three times.

Narina knew it was the agreed signal to Paks that it was either herself or the Lord Chamberlain.

It only took a second before Paks was at the door.

"Is our visitor now decent?" the Lord Chamberlain enquired. "Her Royal Highness wishes to accompany me."

Paks grinned.

"He be in bed, my Lord, and ever so grateful for the comfort of it."

The Lord Chamberlain then strode into the dimly lit room and Narina followed him.

As they moved towards the bed Narina saw that the man she had rescued was propped up against the pillows.

Paks had put a plaster on his forehead where it had been bleeding and there was another one on his cheek.

The Lord Chamberlain reached the side of the bed.

"I hear that you have been rescued by Her Royal Highness and I, as Lord Chamberlain of Alexanderburg, am anxious to hear the story of why you are here."

"Of course, you are," replied the stranger. "And I may say how deeply grateful I am to Her Royal Highness for saving me by a hair's breadth. I can only express my deep gratitude by saying that she behaved with a quickness of intuition I have never encountered before."

Narina stared at him.

Then she and the Lord Chamberlain sat on chairs that Paks had brought to the side of the bed.

"Now first of all, may I ask your name – or is that a secret?"

"It is no secret from you, Lord Chamberlain. My name is Michael Ward."

To her considerable surprise, Narina realised that the Lord Chamberlain stiffened.

Then he exclaimed in sheer astonishment,

"Michael Ward! But naturally I have heard of you. What are you doing here so far from India?"

"If you have heard of me," replied Michael Ward, "that is very much to my disadvantage and explains why I was very nearly captured by the Russians here."

"So I understand, but I am definitely astonished to see you here. When I was in India, the Viceroy told me of some of the missions you had undertaken and the brilliant way the Army was able to circumvent the Russians, thanks entirely to the information you had supplied to them."

"As you will recognise, the least said about where I am the better. At the same time I have been following one particular Russian for two months, but was unfortunate on the outskirts of your country to be recognised by a man I nearly killed two years ago.

"My disguise having been pierced, there was only one thing I could do and that was to run for it. I regret to say the Russians who are trying to catch me have followed me over your frontier and now know I am in the Palace."

"Are there many of them?" the Lord Chamberlain enquired.

"Not enough to worry you at present, but I would certainly double your defences as soon as possible. In fact when I have completed my current task, I was going to see that you are informed that the Russian bear has his eagle eye on you, and they are beginning their usual trickery in an endeavour to take over Alexanderburg."

"I am aware of that already," the Lord Chamberlain replied. "In fact you have come at what may be a fortunate time because, as you could well have guessed, His Royal Highness is away on a secret visit of which no one knows about except myself, the servant who has looked after you, and – Her Royal Highness."

He hesitated before he said the last three words.

Narina realised that he was wondering whether he should tell Michael Ward that Princess Louise was with her husband or leave him thinking that she was Louise.

As if he wished to inform her that the latter was his intention, the Lord Chamberlain looked at her and said,

"I think, Your Royal Highness, it is only right that I should explain to you that the gentleman you have rescued is a member of a very secret band of British Officers who are trying to counter Russian ambitions against India."

Narina smiled.

"I think you are talking about *The Great Game*."

"You have heard about it, Your Royal Highness?" Michael asked.

"My father is a close friend of the Viceroy, Lord Ripon, and he told him in confidence how the information won by members of *The Great Game* had saved the Forts on the North-West frontier and how they brought in reports on what was happening in Asia where the Cossack hordes are riding to victory day after day."

Michael laughed.

"We always imagine that no one but the authorities are aware of our activities, and we flatter ourselves that we get away with it time after time. Yet Your Royal Highness knows our secret!"

"Only second-hand until now!" replied Narina.

"If that made you as quick as you were in taking me to safety, I can only repeat how grateful I am that, thanks entirely to you, I shall live to see the sun rise another day."

Narina gave a little cry.

"I understand what you are saying. But, of course, you are still vulnerable and now they know where you are, they may well try again."

"I am aware of that," he replied looking at the Lord Chamberlain.

"And so am I," said the Lord Chamberlain. "Now I understand who you are and why you are here, I am going to increase our defences of the Palace considerably. But, as you are both aware, no one else except ourselves must have the slightest idea as to why this is necessary."

"No, of course not," Narina responded. "But will Mr. Ward really be safe, or would it be wise to send him away somewhere else?"

"I think he will not only be safe," mused the Lord Chamberlain as if he was thinking it out, "but I also believe that he could be extremely useful to us."

Narina gazed at him in surprise and so did Michael.

"I don't suppose, Mr. Ward," the Lord Chamberlain went on, "that Paks, the servant, has told you that you are being hidden here in His Royal Highness's bed because it is unoccupied. Everyone in the Palace believes that His Royal Highness is lying here suffering from a fall when out riding which has affected his eyes."

"I thought there must be some reason for the lack of sunshine and the dimness in this beautiful room."

"The reason is quite simple, but a complete secret. His Royal Highness is, at the moment, undergoing a small operation in Constantinople. It would be a great mistake, as you will appreciate better than anyone, for the Russians to know that he is not here in the Palace."

"I can understand that, but I feel sure that you have taken every precaution."

"We thought we had until a member of *The Great Game* has come to take his place – "

"You can trust me, that I do promise you."

"I am not only trusting you, Mr. Ward, but I really want you to stay here until His Royal Highness returns."

Michael stared at him in surprise.

"You will be far safer here than anywhere else. No one would know better than you do that the Russians never search openly for their prey if they can possibly avoid it as usually the only way they can be defeated is if the man they are seeking dies."

Narina gave a little cry of horror.

"I am not exaggerating, as Mr. Ward knows. But it will actually make things much easier for us if he is here, and we need not be frightened that by some mischance the Russians learn that not only is His Royal Highness's bed empty, but that he has left the country."

"I can appreciate that. In fact it might be just what the Russians are waiting for. Of course, as I am somewhat exhausted at the moment and there are so many sore places on my body, I am only too delighted to accept your most kind invitation."

"Thank goodness for that. Now I shall be able to sleep more comfortably at night."

"There is only one thing I would very much like to know," Michael enquired, "and that is who is the beautiful lady I thought must be Her Royal Highness."

The Lord Chamberlain gave a laugh.

"Let me introduce and this is equally a great secret, Miss Narina Kenwin, who has most kindly taken over the place of Her Royal Highness Princess Louise."

"I can only say how grateful I am to you," Michael responded. "I never imagined that any woman would be so quick in understanding my position. Most women would have just been frightened of me and run away."

"While you were in India, you must have heard of Miss Kenwin's father," the Lord Chamberlain remarked. "When he was last there, he was a Canon, but since then he has been made the Bishop of St. Albans."

"Of course I have heard of him. In fact I met him once. I was told that he is an extremely brilliant man."

"Then you will not be surprised that his daughter is brilliant too!" the Lord Chamberlain added.

"Now you are both making me feel embarrassed," said Narina. "Although we have jumped one fence, I have an uncomfortable feeling there are a great number of others ahead of us."

"Yes, indeed there are," replied Michael, "but if you and I cannot jump them together then, I will be quite prepared to eat my hat or whatever the expression is."

They all three laughed and the Lord Chamberlain rose to his feet, saying,

"I am going back to tell the General in command of the troops that the Palace Guard is to be doubled and they must be quite certain that no one gets through."

He was silent for a moment.

"If the Russians could dispose of you, Mr. Ward, and

His Royal Highness at the same time, it would be a coup they have been hoping to achieve for a long time."

"They are not doing that badly," he added grimly. "And as you are know their Empire was once two thousand miles from India, but they have lately been decreasing that space by over twenty miles a day."

"As bad as that!" the Lord Chamberlain exclaimed.

"Worse than that, if we count in the Caravan towns and Khanates they have taken over so unscrupulously with very little resistance."

"Now you are making me more scared than I was already," complained Narina. "Surely we are safe here as long as they believe that the Princess on the throne is under the personal patronage of Her Majesty Queen Victoria."

"That is just what we all want to believe," the Lord Chamberlain said before Michael could reply. "Equally if either the Princess or the ruling Prince is absent, they will claim that gives them every right to take over the country."

"Again you are scaring me even more than before," Narina chipped in.

"I can assure you both," declared Michael, "that the Government of India is determined that Russia will never take possession of her. And the Balkans, if they are clever and resolute can also be saved."

"That is not true of all the Principalities – "

Michael smiled.

"It has to be true of this one. Therefore please do increase your defences immediately and as soon as I have had a good night's sleep, I will be able to tell you a great many things I don't believe you are currently aware of."

"I will look forward to that," the Lord Chamberlain answered.

He put his hand on Narina's shoulder.

"Before Mr. Ward goes to sleep, I suggest that you talk to him and reassure yourself that he will act the part we request of him with a brilliance that no one else could."

He sighed before he continued,

"I am hoping that he will be willing to stay here, as you will, until Their Royal Highnesses return. But just as you were yesterday taken by surprise and performed your duty beautifully in Princess Louise's absence, we may have to call on Mr. Ward to do the same thing."

Narina drew in her breath.

Then she looked at Michael to see if he was about to protest.

Even in the dim light of the room she could see that his eyes were twinkling.

"There is one lesson I have learnt in this world," he volunteered, "and that is no one gets anything for nothing. Very well, my Lord Chamberlain, I am at your service, and if I have to play the part of a ruling Prince or a reluctant mule, I am perfectly prepared to do either!"

The Lord Chamberlain chuckled.

"I thought that you would, Mr. Ward, but I can only hope for your sake it will not be necessary. Just remember that for everyone here, you are His Royal Highness Prince Rudolf, who is suffering from an accident while out riding that has threatened his eyesight."

"I will not forget, my Lord Chamberlain, and I am only grateful that I can play the part to help you."

"I will come and see you later this evening and tell you what orders I have given."

The Lord Chamberlain walked towards the door.

As he reached it he turned back to raise his hand.

Then he went out and Narina heard him speaking to Paks, who was keeping watch outside.

As she looked at Michael, she realised that he was extremely tired as he lay back against the pillows.

"I think," she suggested, "you would go to sleep if I left you alone. After all you have been through, you must be completely exhausted."

"I have not been able to sleep at all for the last three nights. I have been moving around in the darkness as that was much safer and I only managed to snatch an hour or two's rest each day in a hayrick or a dry ditch."

"Then you must go to sleep now, Mr. Ward. Shall we wake you up when it is time for dinner to be brought to you here – or would you rather sleep on?"

"I think as I have had very little to eat, I would like to join you for dinner not only because I would very much enjoy something to eat but because I can then talk to you."

"Well, close your eyes and know that you are quite safe, and Paks is always available if you need anything."

Michael smiled at her.

Narina realised that his eyes were slowly closing.

She did not say any more as she walked towards the door and when she reached it and looked back, she had the feeling, although it was difficult to see clearly, that he was already fast asleep.

Outside she found Paks.

She told him that His Royal Highness, as Mr. Ward was now to be called, was to sleep until dinner time.

"He's had a real hard time, that gentleman," Paks muttered. "He's got some nasty gashes on his back and I'll treat them as soon as I can get at him."

"There will be plenty of time for that if he has to stay in bed. If he walks about someone is bound to see him and think he is well enough to come downstairs and then they will recognise him as not being Prince Rudolf."

"You're so very right, Your Royal Highness, and I thinks that already. If you asks me, it's a gift from Heaven having him turn up when I were beginning to think it were dangerous having no one in that bed."

"I thought it was all arranged so that no one would ever know?"

"That's what we planned, but there's always those who be so very curious about a Royal personage and them housemaids who think he's wonderful are always sneaking up hoping to take a peep at him."

"Now they will at least see someone in his bed, so perhaps Mr. Ward is a blessing in disguise."

"If you asks me that's what he be."

Narina went into the sitting room.

As she did so she realised she had left behind in the garden the book her father had given her to read.

'I will go and fetch it,' she decided.

Then suddenly she was afraid.

Those Russians, who had been just behind Michael, would have guessed that he had disappeared into the Palace and they might even have seen her taking him in.

If they took her prisoner, thinking she was Louise, they could make life incredibly difficult and Prince Rudolf would not be there to negotiate for her or to lead the Army of Alexanderburg against them.

'I will send Maria out for it later,' she told herself.

As she sat down at the desk in front of the window of the sitting room, she could not help feeling that it was rather exciting to have Michael Ward to talk to.

Maybe he would be clever enough to come up with new ideas that were badly needed in Alexanderburg.

She had not yet met the Prime Minister, but she had

a feeling, from what she had heard, that he was rather like the Mayor.

He wished to keep things as they always had been rather than to introduce new ideas into the country.

'I am quite sure,' she thought, 'that Michael Ward, as he has been so very successful in *The Great Game*, will think of new ways for Alexanderburg to save itself.'

It was an exciting idea and she glanced at the clock.

She was hoping that the hours would pass quickly so that she could talk to Michael at dinner.

Time did pass slowly before Maria came to tell her that her bath was now ready and as before, it was arranged by the fireplace.

Tonight she went to the wardrobe herself to choose the gown she would wear.

And it was obviously wrong to wear one of the very elaborate ones which hung there, but she found a gown that was, she thought, very attractive. It was more suitable for a dinner *á deux* than if she had been dining in the Royal banqueting room.

Again Maria arranged her hair in the same way that Louise wore it, although it did pass through her mind that it would be more flattering to look like herself.

Yet it was likely that the Lord Chamberlain would drop in after dinner, and she felt that she must play her part in pretending to be Louise exactly as she had promised to do before the Royal couple had disappeared in the dark of the night to Constantinople.

Paks had orders to wake Mr. Ward and he had said to Narina before he went in to do so,

"I ain't allowing that Ward gentleman to get up for dinner, Your Royal Highness. He has to stay where he be until them wounds on his back have been properly treated.

Even then there be no point in him a-getting up and finding them starts to bleed again."

"No, Paks, you are quite right and if he wants to go on sleeping I will understand. Otherwise I suggest you put a table by the bed and I can sit on one side of it."

It was the way she had had meals with her mother when she was ill and she had always thought it was a cosy and delightful way to eat for someone in bed.

She waited until Paks came to the sitting room to announce rather pompously,

"Dinner be served, Your Royal Highness."

Narina jumped up and went into the bedroom.

The curtains were drawn although it was still fairly light outside and candles were lit.

Narina knew that everything that happened upstairs was promptly known downstairs.

If there were too many candles being lit they would never believe that Prince Rudolf was in the darkness the doctors had ordered for him.

There was, however, just one small candelabrum on the table and Narina was not surprised to find that it was composed of cupids with stars at their feet.

The tablecloth was of very fine lace and Paks had arranged bright flowers from the garden on the table.

Michael was sitting up in bed with his hair neatly brushed and wearing a silk scarf round his neck.

He looked, she thought, very much better than he had before he had gone to sleep.

He smiled as she walked across the room.

"I must tell you," he said as she sat down, "that you look exceedingly beautiful and very smart. As this is the first decent meal I have had for many months, I am going to enjoy every mouthful. But most of all I will appreciate the beauty I will share it with."

"That makes it exciting for me too," Narina replied, "and if you are looking forward to dinner then so am I. I have found it very gloomy eating alone and having no one to talk to except for Paks."

"He is exactly the sort of servant who should be in charge of a Royal Prince and he made me laugh even when he was hurting me when treating my wounds."

"Are they still very uncomfortable?"

"I am not going to think about that while you are here. I want you to tell all me about yourself and how you could turn up so unexpectedly when I would expect you to be at home helping your father to teach the children their Catechism."

Narina laughed.

"I do not have to do that, but I am alone with Papa most of the time. He is a wonderful companion when he is not too busy to attend to me."

"So then you were unexpectedly caught up in this wildly dramatic adventure, because, I would guess, you are a friend of Princess Louise and also resemble her."

"That is very astute of you. We were always taken for twins at school, although actually we are not related. When Louise asked me to come out here at a moment's notice, I came with pleasure although I had no idea what was expected of me."

"I think it is very brave of you – "

"It is the most exciting and thrilling thing that has ever happened to me except when someone like you comes out of the blue and scares me half to death!"

"I am sorry if I scared you, but you were just like an angel delivering me from the devil and carrying me on winged feet to safety."

Narina giggled.

"You will really have to write a book about it one day including all your own adventures in India."

"I have thought of that, but actually it will not be very long before I am forced to retire."

"Forced!" exclaimed Narina.

"For family reasons for one thing and for another, as you have learnt today, I am now recognised by too many people. However well I disguise myself, the Russians soon will no longer be deceived."

"What disguise were you in when you came here?"

"When I left India from the North-West Frontier, I was a Holy Man. When I came further west, I was a native selling horses, having picked up the two I had with me on a battlefield."

"I think it is all so very very brave of you," Narina remarked admiringly.

"It is very thrilling, exciting and usually terrifying, especially when I wonder how many minutes I have left to live."

Narina drew in her breath.

"How can you be so brave as to go on fighting what might easily be a losing battle?"

"I am well aware of that possibility, but at the same time I am pitting my brains against the Russian brains and I like to think mine are sharper than theirs."

They both laughed at his unexpected explanation.

"You must be very glad tonight that at least you can sleep without being afraid."

"It is even better to have met you," replied Michael. "I am still thinking of you as an angel sent from Heaven to save me, and I am quite certain that for the moment at any rate, looking as you do now, you are not acting a part."

Because he spoke so seriously, Narina blushed.

She had no idea how exquisitely and delightfully lovely she was looking as she did so.

CHAPTER FIVE

The next morning Paks knocked on Narina's door to say that he wished to speak to her.

She told him to come in and he then announced,

"Mr. Ward be not very well today. The exhaustion after what he's been through has caught up with him."

"Oh, is he ill?" Narina asked apprehensively.

Paks shook his head.

"Not really ill. He just needs to sleep and that's a better medicine than any doctor can give him."

"Absolutely, Paks. I remember my father saying, when he had been climbing a mountain or something like that, he would sleep and sleep until he felt himself again."

"That, Your Royal Highness, is precisely what our patient be doing. You see he'll come bouncing back and be himself again in a very short time."

"His wounds are now healing?"

"They be better, but they be painful when he thinks about them."

He picked up Narina's breakfast tray and took it out of the room.

As she could not ride in the mornings as she did at home Narina found it easier to stay in bed for breakfast and dress afterwards.

She still felt nervous about going into the garden.

Although she did laugh at herself for being scared,

she could still see the blood on Michael's face as he came out from the trees.

The Lord Chamberlain assured her the guard round the Palace had been doubled with more sentries posted at night, as well as Officers keeping watch for any Russians who might be lurking about.

Even so Narina could not help feeling worried.

She thought it so sensible of Michael to sleep away his fears and stress.

It had, however, left her with little to do, so once again she turned to her father's book for consolation.

She was reading by the open window in her sitting room when the Lord Chamberlain entered.

She jumped up eagerly to welcome him.

"I was hoping you would come to see me today, as our patient is asleep and I have no one to talk to."

"Well now you are going to hear some rather bad news," the Lord Chamberlain responded.

Narina looked at him anxiously.

"What is it?" she asked.

It flashed through her mind that perhaps it was bad news from Constantinople.

Had Prince Rudolf's operation not been a success?

It was almost a relief when he replied,

"We have an unwelcome visitor."

"Unwelcome?" queried Narina.

The Lord Chamberlain nodded and then sat down.

"You may have heard of him, but he is known as a mischief-maker, and the last thing we want at this moment is him sneaking round to find out what is going on."

"Who can it be?"

"Prince Hans von Vechtel,"

The name meant nothing to her, so she commented,

"The name sounds German."

"He is German in a way, although he tends to vary his nationality to suit whichever country he is in."

Narina gave a laugh.

"He sounds rather amusing. Tell me about him."

"It is not very amusing to us, because we have to be even more careful than we are at the moment not to let him know that Their Royal Highnesses are not here."

"You mean that I must not see him – "

"No, that is not important," the Lord Chamberlain said. "He has never met Princess Louise, because the last time he came to stay was over two years ago when she and the Prince were on their honeymoon in the Summer Palace and naturally they received no visitors."

"So why are you upset that he is here now? After all, he cannot see His Royal Highness."

"But he will undoubtedly try and even so it would not matter particularly, as he has not seen Prince Rudolf for many years and therefore would not suspect that Michael Ward is impersonating him."

"Then I do not understand, Lord Chamberlain, why you are so worried about this visitor."

He settled himself more comfortably in the chair.

"He is, as I have already said, a trouble-maker. He goes from country to country finding out their weak spots and talks about them to other countries, often amusingly, but invariably dangerously."

"And why should he do that?"

"Because he wants to be thought important. His is a small Principality on the borders of Russia and Germany.

They argued about which country his Principality belonged to when Bismarck created the German Empire. As far as I know, they are still arguing about it!"

"It sounds too extraordinary."

"What you will find more extraordinary or perhaps, like most women, exciting, is Prince Hans himself – "

"Tell me about him, please," begged Narina.

"Well in the first place, you will certainly find him very good-looking and to all intents and purposes he is an amusing guest. But I am quite convinced in my own mind that he has come here so that he can tell the Russians why there is not yet an heir to the throne."

Narina gave a cry of protest as he continued,

"If he thinks there is any other reason for it except a natural one, he will undoubtedly make a good deal out of it and have the Czar listening to every word he has to say."

Narina started to realise that the Lord Chamberlain was not exaggerating that Prince Hans was dangerous.

After a moment she remarked,

"Surely, as far as he knows, Prince Rudolf cannot meet him and I am constantly at his bedside. Therefore he cannot expect to meet him or me."

"That is what I would like to say, but it would be a mistake."

"Why?" enquired Narina.

"Because he would then be quite sure that there was something odd going on. We can say, as we have already, that Prince Rudolf has had an accident which has affected his sight, but you are hale and hearty and so you can hardly refuse to entertain such an important guest as the Prince."

Narina would have protested, but he carried on,

"You are the only person who can reassure him that there is nothing unusual happening here at present."

"Suppose he does not believe me?" Narina asked in a very small voice.

The Lord Chamberlain smiled.

"You are very beautiful as you must realise and the Prince has a distinct penchant for beautiful women. You merely have to flatter him a little and tell him how pleased you are to meet him and I would not mind betting quite a considerable sum that he will be at your feet."

"But suppose he insists on seeing Prince Rudolf?"

"If we are forced to take him into the sick room and the Prince is asleep with the sunlight excluded, he cannot think there is anything unusual or suspicious about that."

"I do see your point, Lord Chamberlain, but you are quite certain that I must entertain him?"

"Of course you must. I have arranged for a dinner to be held in the Palace tonight to which I have invited the Prime Minister and his wife, as well as a young Statesman with his very pretty wife he married only a short time ago."

"Is that all?"

"It is quite enough. I do not want to include a large number of guests, who might by some mischance just say something which would make him suspect that things are not as entirely peaceful in this country as we pretend."

Narina looked at him in a startled way.

"Are you saying the Russians are creating trouble?"

"Not openly, but there are rumours that in outlying villages they are trying to stir up dissatisfaction. Although we cannot pinpoint it, we are aware that it is happening."

"And you think that this Prince Hans will report to the Russians that their agents are being successful?"

"Undoubtedly, if he thinks it is significant enough, and as you must know, Russia has, for a long time, wanted Alexanderburg to be joined to them."

"It is most unfortunate that you actually border on Russian territory,"

"That is what I have often thought myself, but there is nothing we can do about it except fight desperately with every possible weapon to retain our independence."

He spoke with a tone in his voice that told Narina how much it meant to him.

She knew if anyone had to sacrifice his life to save Alexanderburg it would be the Lord Chamberlain.

"I will do everything you want me to do, but please don't let me make mistakes. It would be ghastly if I was responsible for letting the enemy into our midst."

"That is what I often feel myself, so I want you to be as pleasant as you can manage to Prince Hans tonight. He will flirt with you, as he always flirts with every pretty woman he comes into contact with."

"How old is he?" enquired Narina.

"Getting on for thirty-five. I believe he was a terror when he was a child and has not changed since he grew up. He is a gossip-monger who loves to stir up trouble, but it would be dangerous to underestimate him."

"What does he gain by behaving like this?"

"Power and influence. He adores both and he has in his own peculiar way made himself quite important to a number of countries. I am told that the Czarina dotes on him and makes a huge fuss of him whenever he visits St. Petersburg."

"And you think he has a special reason for coming to Alexanderburg now?"

He paused before responding,

"Perhaps I am being imaginative and overly ultra-sensitive, but he is the very last person I would welcome to the Palace now. Yet it is impossible to keep him away."

"I promise you I will do my best to help. Just tell me what I must do and I will be very careful what I say."

"The one thing he is *not* to find out, is that you are taking the place of Her Royal Highness and that Michael Ward, of all people, is actually in Prince Rudolf's bed."

He gave a laugh with no humour in it.

"It would be a tale to sweep across the dinner tables of Europe and the Russians would use it as a key to open the door and let themselves into this country."

"So what do you want me to do, Lord Chaberlain?"

"I want you first to come downstairs for luncheon, at which there will be no guests and then you can talk to Prince Hans, or rather listen to him, without interruption."

"You are quite certain he has never seen Louise?"

"He has never set eyes on her to my knowledge, but he does know that she is English and will therefore not be suspicious that you are play-acting. What he really wants to know is why you have not yet produced an heir to the throne, and if our Army is as small and as ineffective as it is reputed to be amongst some of the other Balkan States who are jealous of us."

"Surely, Lord Chamberlain, you can easily increase the size of your Army."

She was thinking of the large number of men she had seen walking in the streets not in uniform as she drove into the City.

Now she thought about it, very few of the women she had talked to had said their husband was a soldier.

"I have been advocating for some time that all the young men in the country should be encouraged to join the Army if only for just a few years so that they would learn to fight and that might in time be very necessary."

"And so then who is preventing it?"

"The Prime Minister for one. He is persuading the Cabinet and Members of Parliament that if we have a large Army we might seem to be aggressive and our neighbours might believe that we are threatening *them*."

"But surely they do understand that the real threat comes from Russia?" exclaimed Narina.

"They believe all they want to believe and they are completely and absolutely certain that as we are now ruled by an English Princess, we are perfectly safe."

Narina gave a deep sigh.

"I appreciate all you are feeling. It is just what my father has told me happened in India. For a long time they refused to believe there was any threat from the Russians."

"Exactly and their defences are still, I am told, not as complete as they should be."

"If they were, we would not need men like Michael Ward to risk their lives in *The Great Game*."

"No, of course not. I only wish we had something like that here. The majority of the people are complacent and convinced that we need not be afraid."

"Then that is just the sort of thing that Prince Hans must not find out."

The Lord Chamberlain nodded.

"What you have to do," he suggested, "is keep his mind on a more attractive subject, which is *yourself*."

"I will do my best," smiled Narina.

After the Lord Chamberlain had left her, she longed to go into the closed bedroom and tell Michael Ward what was happening.

When she asked Paks, he insisted that he was still asleep and under no circumstances should he be disturbed.

Narina changed her gown.

She chose one of the prettiest and most fashionable belonging to Louise. She added some attractive jewellery and put two strings of pearls round her neck.

There were pearl earrings to match and a diamond bracelet which was narrow enough not to seem ostentatious in the daytime.

Then feeling her heart was beating rather heavily in case she made a mistake, she walked down the stairs.

She entered the reception room in which she was to meet Prince Hans before luncheon.

She learnt from one of the *aides-de-camp* that the Lord Chamberlain and the General commanding the troops had been showing Prince Hans the best horses in the Royal Cavalry stables.

Narina was certain this was an astute way to show him something of the Army itself, but she merely smiled and asked the *aide-de-camp*,

"Was His Royal Highness driving particularly fine horses?"

"Very fine indeed, Your Royal Highness," the *aide-de-camp* replied with a note of envy in his voice. "Prince Hans does everything in style, bringing extra horses with him in case any should go lame and an attendance of eight servants."

Narina laughed as she thought it so funny.

She could scarcely imagine any Englishman going about with such pomp and ceremony.

From the way the *aide-de-camp* spoke she was sure it all made Prince Hans, in other people's eyes, much more impressive than he actually was.

She had not been in the reception room for more than a few minutes before the *aide-de-camp* accompanied by Prince Hans entered the room.

"You must forgive us, Your Royal Highness," he said to Narina, "if we are late, but His Royal Highness has been making an inspection of our Cavalry horses and has been most complimentary about them."

"I am delighted to meet Your Royal Highness, and to welcome you to the Palace," Narina addressed him.

She held out her hand and Prince Hans raised her hand in the French fashion and murmured,

"Your Royal Highness is even more beautiful than I was told you were."

"I am only glad to see that Your Royal Highness is not disappointed," Narina managed to reply.

When they went into luncheon, they were joined by two equerries, who had met the Prince on his last visit and he was most gracious to them.

As luncheon began he started talking and Narina could see why in many ways he was almost hypnotic.

He was amusing, witty, and at the same time he had a sharp dig at everyone and everything he spoke about.

Yet because it was like learning history that was not in books, she found the conversation fascinating.

He paid Narina endless compliments in between all the catty remarks he was making about other Rulers, even the Czar himself.

Alexander III was already being talked about as one of the most frightening Czars Russia had ever produced.

Narina had heard her father expound the theory that although the Balkans had been frightened of Alexander II, he possessed many of the attributes of a fine Ruler.

On the morning of his death he was working on a reform which would have launched Russia irrevocably into the modern world – it was the granting of a Parliamentary Charter.

When he was later murdered, every house, balcony, window and lampstand was draped in black.

Narina could recall that the first act of the new Czar Alexander III was to tear up the unfinished manifesto lying on his father's desk.

She had learnt since she arrived in Alexanderburg that Alexander III was already more feared by the world than any other Czar before him.

If the Russians had been frightening before to their victims, they were doubly terrifying now.

She only wished that she had asked her father more about the convoluted political situation in the Balkans.

And now this good-looking Prince was deliberately poking fun at the Czar, who was beginning to terrorise all of Eastern Europe.

Then unexpectedly the Prince changed his tune and looked Narina full in the face.

"You must now tell me all about yourself, beautiful Princess," he began. "In fact, as I am so overwhelmed by your beauty, I have had difficulty in thinking of anything else, least of all the troubles of Russia."

"But you know that we are interested, Your Royal Highness," the Lord Chamberlain chipped in.

"You will learn what is going to occur without my telling you about it," the Prince replied blithely, "and now, because your flowers are famed throughout all the Balkan States, I would like Her Royal Highness to take me into the garden so that I can admire them."

It was quite obvious he did not want anyone else to accompany them.

She gave the Lord Chamberlain a despairing look.

There was, however, nothing that Narina could do but accompany the Prince as an equerry opened a door into the garden.

They did not go into the private garden, but into a larger garden that was just as lovely, and because she had wanted to keep out of sight, Narina had only peeped at it through the upstairs windows.

Now as she moved over the grass with Prince Hans beside her, she thought nothing could be more beautiful.

The flowers were of every conceivable colour and there was again a profusion of the white lilies she loved.

"This is just the right setting for you," Prince Hans was saying.

They had talked in almost every language during luncheon – varying from the language of Alexanderburg, which much to her surprise the Prince spoke quite easily, to French and German.

Now he was talking to her in English with a fluency which told her that he was more intelligent than she wanted to believe.

"Are you enjoying yourself in this very small part of the big world?" he asked. "Personally I think you are wasting your beauty on such a trifling audience when you might have one which is worldwide!"

Narina laughed.

"I am quite content and naturally am so very happy with my husband, Rudolf."

"The Lord Chamberlain has told me that I cannot see him, but as I came here specially to do so, I just cannot believe that you will not smuggle me into his bedroom – "

Narina shook her head vigorously.

"No, Your Royal Highness, that would be wrong. His doctors have said he is to have complete rest after his fall and remain in darkness. It is frightening to think that his sight might be ruined forever."

She felt as she spoke that she was admirably acting the part of an anxious wife.

"I have no wish to upset you, and if I really cannot see Rudolf now, I can always come again another day."

"Of course you can, and, I assure you, you will be very welcome," exclaimed Narina.

"*To you*?" Prince Hans enquired.

They had now reached a small lake and there was a wooden seat under the trees.

Without making a comment, as if they both had the same thought at the same time, they sat down.

Prince Hans lent his arm on the back of the seat and moved nearer to Narina.

"Now do tell me about yourself, beautiful one, I am overcome, in fact bewildered, to find anything so exquisite in Alexanderburg, which I always thought a dull country."

"Oh, you must not say that, the people are charming and as they love Rudolf, they are delighted he is so happy."

"I heard you were making him happy. I also heard that you were extremely clever in winning over the women by paying attention to their tiresome children."

"Now how could you have heard that already?"

"I hear everything," Prince Hans crowed loftily. "I am a mine of information on all subjects and I am aware of many events that are going to occur a long time before the newspapers print it in headlines."

He spoke so positively that Narina laughed.

"Now you are asking me to believe that you are not human?"

"Of course I am human. Human enough to find you entrancing and to *long* to touch your lips with mine!"

Narina turned her head away.

"You know as well as I do, Your Royal Highness, you should not talk to me like that."

Prince Hans chortled.

"Whoever can stop me admiring the most beautiful woman I have ever set eyes on and what beautiful woman does not want to hear the truth about herself?"

"Maybe I am the exception, but you make me feel shy and embarrassed."

"I adore you when you are shy and I am finding my visit to Alexanderburg so different from my expectations."

"What did you expect, Your Royal Highness?"

"To enjoy talking to Rudolf and to be bored by his English wife who I was expecting to be rather dumpy and not unlike Queen Victoria!"

Narina laughed because she could not help it.

"How can you be so ridiculous? Rudolf would not marry anyone like that."

"And he was astute enough and fortunate enough to find you. How could you have met each other, if it had not been through the heavy hand of Britain pushing you, as so many others have been pushed, onto a Balkan throne?"

"It is where I am very happy to be," replied Narina stubbornly and in what she hoped was a dignified tone.

"You must look so adorable on it and undoubtedly every man in this little country, unless he is blind, will fall in love with you. How do you expect to keep them at bay?"

"Rudolf will do that for me."

"But just for the moment you and I are alone – "

Prince Hans did not move, but she had the distinct impression that he was about to kiss her.

She rose to her feet.

"Come and see the lake," she suggested. "It is very lovely."

For a moment he did not move, but merely laughed.

"You are running away," he smirked sardonically, "but I promise you, my adorable beautiful Goddess from Olympus, that I am a past master at getting what I want in love – and I never take 'no' for an answer."

Narina could not respond to this assertion, so she pretended not to hear him.

She walked a little way ahead towards the lake and Prince Hans followed her.

Then as they stood looking down at the sunlit water he proposed,

"I would love to take you out swimming, not here where we can be seen, but in the sea where you would look like a mermaid rising from the foam. I could hold you in my arms without the barrier of that gown between us."

"Now you are just speculating about something that could *never* happen and I think, Your Royal Highness, that we should walk back to the Palace, because I am sure that the Lord Chamberlain has much more to show you."

"If it is a question of more horses, then naturally I will have to show an interest in them. But it is still early in the day and if we are to dine together, as I hope we shall do, I shall have a lot to say to you when dinner is finished."

He smiled before he added,

"And that is a promise, not a threat!"

"If you frighten me," answered Narina, "I will run away and hide in Rudolf's room, even though I do not wish to disturb him."

"Ever since I was a boy I have enjoyed a chase for what I desired and I claim without boasting that invariably I win, conquer or steal whatever I want."

They had reached the Palace by now and therefore Narina did not have to reply.

The Lord Chamberlain was waiting for them and he said as they entered the hall,

"We are standing ready for Your Royal Highness's inspection. And you are riding, as I thought Your Royal Highness would wish, on one of your own horses."

"You are most kind," Prince Hans answered.

Then as Narina stood back for him to pass, he took her hand in his and actually touched it with his lips.

"*Au revoir*, my most beautiful Goddess."

As he went off with the Lord Chamberlain, Narina ran up the stairs.

She was hoping that Michael Ward would be awake and that she could talk to him.

When she entered her own part of the Palace, Paks was waiting for her.

"His Royal Highness be still asleep," he said before she could ask, "and I'm a-thinking he'll sleep for another twenty-four hours at least."

Narina felt her spirits drop as she was hoping that Michael would be able to tell her how best to behave with the impetuous Prince.

Prince Hans was indeed different from anyone else she had ever met and she was now beginning to recognise why he was welcomed by every country he visited,

Although he could be a definite danger because he was so indiscreet.

She thought it would be interesting to hear more about the new Czar, who was already spoken about with so much awe and horror, as she had not talked to anyone yet who had actually met him.

At the same time she had a feeling that dinner was going to be a very difficult meal unless the Prince attached himself to the young attractive wife the Lord Chamberlain had spoken about.

She next spent the rest of the afternoon alone in her sitting room attempting to read her book but finding herself continually thinking about Prince Hans.

She never imagined that anyone, even in a novel, could be in any way like him – he was certainly not a man one expected to meet in real life.

*

When it was time to dress for dinner, she chose a pretty but elaborate gown belonging to Louise.

She had not expected to wear it unless there was a large party or she had to attend an official engagement.

Because it was important occasion, she chose a lot of Louise's jewellery to wear with the gown – not because she wanted to glitter, but she wanted Prince Hans to realise that she was the devoted wife of the reigning Prince.

And therefore he should not be so familiar with her.

She added a small diamond tiara and a necklace of the same stones around her neck.

She felt she looked not only Regal but rather older and someone who should be treated with respect.

As she walked downstairs to dinner, she suddenly recalled that she was due to meet the Prime Minister for the first time and he might, if he was perceptive, realise that she was not Princess Louise.

When she entered the reception room where they were waiting for her, she noticed that the Prime Minister was wearing dark spectacles.

That, of course, was another reason why the clever Lord Chamberlain had invited him to dinner rather than a younger man, and his wife as well appeared to have trouble with her eyes.

She curtsied low as Narina welcomed her.

The other couple were not at all interesting and she thought the wife of the Statesman was indeed pretty, but in a somewhat unoriginal way.

It was quite obvious to Narina that Prince Hans had eyes only for herself and he had no intention of wasting his conversation or his wit on anyone else.

It was hopeless to make him do anything he did not wish to do, and he talked to her all through dinner and he made her laugh and occasionally blush at his compliments.

The rest of the guests were merely an audience for his performance – just occasionally he looked at them as if he expected them to applaud!

Then he would turn to Narina to dazzle her with his descriptions of the parties he had attended in all parts of Europe.

He made scandalous allegations about practically everyone of any importance and there was no doubt that all the things he said were unkind and most of them untrue.

But the way he said them and the quick turn of his wit was, she thought, so amusing that it was impossible to rebuke him, even though he pilloried Queen Victoria and was sarcastic about the British Government.

In fact dinner passed remarkably quickly.

Narina could hardly believe it was true when the Prime Minister said he was too old to stay up late and bade everyone goodnight and the other couple, who had hardly opened their mouths, followed his example.

As the equerry showed them to the door, the Lord Chamberlain turned to Prince Hans,

"I expect, Your Royal Highness, after quite a long day, you are prepared to retire to bed."

"Yes, indeed, and as I am in the same room that I occupied the last time I came here, there is no need for you to escort me up the stairs. If I am not mistaken, Her Royal Highness is on the same floor."

There was nothing the Lord Chamberlain could do but to bid him goodnight.

Narina and Prince Hans walked up the stairs side by side.

"Now at last," he whispered, "I can talk to you as I want to talk to you and to tell you how, as soon as we met, my heart turned a somersault. I have the distinct feeling I have fallen in love."

"That would be a very silly thing to do!"

"How could I possibly help it? Love is irresistible, and who can resist it when it comes into our lives?"

"You are right about that, and that is just what I feel about Rudolf. It is very sad that he is not well enough for you to meet him."

"I am content to see you, but, my lovely one, you must now console me for not having the pleasure of seeing my old friend, Rudolf, and make me happy as only you can do at this very moment."

"I can only hope that you will sleep well," Narina answered, "and be ready in the morning to visit the many points of interest the Lord Chamberlain has organised for you."

"I am not concerned about the morning, but about *tonight*."

They had by now reached the top of the stairs and were walking along the corridor to the Royal Apartments.

It was then with a sense of relief, as she was afraid of what he might say or do next, that Narina saw Paks.

He was standing like a sentinel outside the door of Prince Rudolf's bedroom.

Prince Hans's room, as she had already ascertained, was several doors away.

The door was open and she could see there was a valet inside waiting for the Prince.

Narina stopped and turned to Prince Hans,

"Good night, Your Royal Highness. I am hoping you will sleep comfortably and not be disturbed."

His eyes were twinkling as they looked into hers.

He was holding her hand and crushing her fingers as he did so.

"*Au revoir*, my beautiful Goddess – and it really is just *au revoir*."

He turned round and walked into his room without looking back.

As he closed the door, Narina sighed.

'I have won that battle,' she thought to herself and walked towards Paks.

"Is His Royal Highness asleep?" she asked.

"Yes, but I thinks he might wake up later. So I left him some lemonade and biscuits. If you hears him moving around it might be that one of his wounds is a-hurting him. If you ring the bell, it'll wake me at once."

"I hope it will not be necessary, Paks, but naturally I will go to him if I think he needs me."

Paks looked down the corridor to the room Prince Hans was occupying.

"I shouldn't come outside, if I be you, Your Royal Highness, there be a communicating-door, as I expects you knows, in your bedroom."

Narina gave a start.

"Oh, yes, Maria did tell me something about it, but I have not used it yet."

"Well if I were you," said Paks, "I'd lock your door afore you goes to bed and, if you wants to see His Royal Highness, then go in through the communicating-door."

"I will do that, Paks, and thank you for telling me."

She smiled at him and then went to her room where Maria was waiting for her.

"You looked so lovely tonight, Lady," cried Maria. "Everyone downstairs was a-talking about you and saying they've never seen Her Royal Highness look better. They was ever so certain it must be because you was expecting a child!"

"Oh, Maria, I do so hope that's true, not for me, but for Princess Louise."

"I've a feeling in me bones that everything'll be all right and it's not often the Lord God ignores *my* prayers."

"I am praying too and it will be wonderful when they tell us you are right and all is as it ought to be."

"That's exactly what I'm a-hoping too."

Narina hung her pretty dress up in the wardrobe and put the jewellery away in its velvet box.

When she had washed and was ready to climb into bed, Maria said,

"I'll be calling you at eight o'clock tomorrow as I expects you'll be breakfasting with His Royal Highness once he wakes."

For a moment Narina thought she was talking about Prince Hans and then she realised Maria meant Michael.

"Yes, indeed, I would love to have breakfast with him. I only hope he is awake by then."

"If not, you can always go downstairs and have it with Prince Hans and from what I hears he's over the moon about you!"

"I do hope he will be leaving tomorrow."

She thought as she was speaking that it would be a good thing if he did, but equally if she was honest she had found him most amusing and interesting when he was not paying her exaggerated compliments.

She went to the window as she did on most nights.

She pulled back both the curtains to gaze out at the moonlight flooding over the garden.

Once again the view was like a fairy story and she stood for some time thinking how lovely it all was.

Then she turned back into the room.

Maria had blown out all the candles except for the little gold candelabrum by her bed.

As she reached it, she remembered she must lock her door and walked towards it.

Then she saw to her astonishment that the key was not there as it had been every night previously.

Although she thought it unnecessary she had locked the door in case anyone should look in and realise that she was sleeping in the Blue Room and not with Prince Rudolf.

Now a frightening thought suddenly struck her.

It was most unlikely that Maria had taken away the key and there was only one other person who might have done so.

She remembered the way that Prince Hans had said *au revoir* to her and not goodnight.

She turned back and ran to the communicating-door which was near the window.

On it was hung an elaborate mirror which made it unnoticeable to anyone unaware of it.

She opened the door.

Then as she came rushing into the Royal bedroom, she realised that Michael was awake.

"You come to say goodnight to me?" he asked.

She ran to the side of his bed.

"I have come to say that I must stay here tonight," she said in a frightened little voice. "Because the key is not in my door."

He looked at her in surprise.

"I will sleep on the sofa. I am not afraid of one of the Palace servants spying on us, but of Prince Hans."

"Are you telling me that *he* is staying here?"

"Yes, he arrived this morning and although I cannot believe it, he said *au revoir* to me just now in a meaningful way instead of goodnight."

"I can well believe it. He pursues every attractive woman and as, you have undoubtedly found, he hypnotises them into believing that he is really in love with them."

"I do not believe anything of the sort. He has been extremely complimentary to me, but the Lord Chamberlain insisted that I was to please him and it would be a mistake to quarrel with him."

"He is speaking good sense indeed."

Narina looked back at the door through which she had just come.

"Shall I go back," she asked, "and bring a blanket or can you spare one of yours?"

Michael smiled.

"This bed is very large and if you are going to act a part, you should act it properly."

Narina stared at him.

"I don't – understand," she stammered hesitatingly.

"I will promise not to upset you or ever make you embarrassed, but if, as we suspect, Prince Hans is looking for you and is determined to find out what our relationship really is, then the only way out is for you to trust me."

"I am – afraid that I will make you uncomfortable."

"I promise you will not do so and if you think that someone might be creeping into our room at any moment, I suggest we stop arguing about it and you get into bed now and blow out the candles."

As he spoke, he lunged as far away as he could to the far side of the bed, which was indeed a very large one.

As Narina gingerly crept in and lay on her side, she was aware there was a large gap between her and Michael.

At the same time she thought that nothing could be more embarrassing – *she was sharing a bed with a man she had only just met!*

"Blow out the candles now," he whispered, "I think I hear a movement next door."

Narina did as she was told.

As she lay back against the pillows, she thought he must have very acute hearing as there was no sound as far as she could ascertain.

Then as they both lay stiff and listening, very very slowly the door into Prince Rudolf's room began to open.

She had not blown out the candles by her bed in the other room and although it was very faint because the room was so large, there was a perceptible streak of light coming in through the communicating-door.

She lay absolutely still in the bed and then Michael turned to Narina and said in a low voice which was only just audible,

"My darling, my sweet, how could I have neglected you by sleeping all day? You know I want you with me and there is so much we have to do together."

Narina did not understand what was happening.

Then she felt Michael's hand pressing on her bare arm and it told her without words that she had to reply.

"I did not want to wake you," she murmured, "but I have missed you so much all day."

"Now I will tell you how much I have missed you, my sweetest – "

They both noticed that for a split second the streak of light from the communicating-door clouded over.

It was as if someone had peeped into the room.

Then just as softly as it had opened, the door closed again and the light was no longer there.

Michael and Narina did not speak or move.

Then Michael said with a distinct hint of laughter in his voice,

"Once again we have defeated the enemy and rather cleverly!"

CHAPTER SIX

For a moment there was silence.

Then Narina asked in a rather frightened tone,

"Shall I go back to my own room now?"

"No, of course not," replied Michael. "If the key is missing, there is every chance he will return later to make quite sure he was not imagining all he heard just now."

"But I cannot stay here and be a nuisance to you – "

"I don't think 'nuisance' is the right word, although I think I would find it very uncomfortable sleeping on the sofa, if you insist you cannot share this bed with me, that is what I will have to do."

"But – you cannot – want me in your bed – "

It was a moment before Michael replied and then with laughter in his voice he said,

"That is a question I must not answer, but I suggest we make the best of this comfortable bed. And if you are worried that I will embarrass you, I will place one of these pillows between us."

He took a pillow from behind his head and placed it down the middle of the bed.

Then he suggested very quietly,

"Go to sleep. You have been putting up with that tiresome Prince Hans all day and you can now forget about him and hope that nothing else happens until morning."

"You are so kind and understanding – "

Michael did not answer.

He merely turned his back on Narina.

Because she thought it was embarrassing to go on discussing it, Narina too turned away and closed her eyes.

She did not expect to sleep, but it had been a long day with so much anxiety in it.

*

She was sleeping peacefully when to her surprise Michael woke her up.

"It is half-past six," he whispered, "and I think you should now go back to your own room in case Maria and Paks start asking us any questions."

"Yes, of course," agreed Narina. "I hope that you slept well and I did not disturb you."

"Shall I say I slept as well as could be expected! Now hurry in case Paks appears early."

Narina slipped out of the bed.

It seemed to her extraordinary that she had slept all night beside a man she really did not know and yet had not been afraid or embarrassed.

Then as she reached the foot of the bed she stopped.

"Thank you very very much for being so kind," she breathed. "I only wish that I did not have to see that Prince Hans again today."

"Behave as if nothing has happened, just remember that he is the one who is frustrated and has had the Gates of Paradise closed abruptly on him!"

Because it was such an unexpected thing for him to have said, Narina gave a little laugh.

Then she opened the communicating-door and went into her own room.

Maria called her at eight o'clock.

Narina anticipated that she would be bringing in her breakfast and sat up in bed.

But Maria muttered,

"Paks has just received an urgent message from the Lord Chamberlain to say that he wishes to see you as soon as you are dressed and ready to receive him."

Narina wondered what had happened, but there was nothing she could do but dress as quickly as possible.

At half-past eight she walked into her sitting room where her breakfast was waiting for her.

She helped herself to fish that she knew must have come out of the sea that very morning.

The door opened and the Lord Chamberlain came into the room.

"Good morning, Your Royal Highness."

Narina smiled at him.

"What has happened?" she asked him nervously.

"Something rather serious and I want your advice before talking to our invalid next door."

Narina's eyes widened.

She put down her knife and fork and was ready to listen attentively to the Lord Chamberlain.

"Prince Hans sent me a message early this morning, saying he would like to inspect a Parade of our troops."

"He has asked for a Parade!" cried Narina. "You know that whatever he sees will be reported straight back to your enemies."

"To refuse him, however, would not only appear to be rude, but would convince him that things are worse than they really are."

"Then what are you going to do?"

"I want, if at all possible, for Michael Ward to take the salute and play the part of Prince Rudolf!"

Narina stared at the Lord Chamberlain.

"You really want that?" she cried. "But surely the people will recognise immediately that he is an imposter."

"That is why I am consulting you, although I know that you have only seen Prince Rudolf for a moment or so. Do you think that if he wears glasses and a bandage round his head, the people would realise that the man in uniform and a feathered hat, as is traditional here, is not the Prince to whom they owe their allegiance?"

Narina drew in her breath.

She could understand that it was a difficult problem and a very worrying one for the Lord Chamberlain.

But equally she realised there was a resemblance between the two of them and it might easily deceive those intent on observing the Alexanderburg soldiers.

To begin with they were the same height.

They both had an English look about them.

The only important difference apart from their eyes, which could be covered, was the colour of their hair.

She realised the Lord Chamberlain was waiting.

"I rather think," she began, "although I am terrified of getting it wrong, that if Michael's hair was darkened and he wears dark glasses and Prince Rudolf's uniform, no one could suspect that the real Prince was not him."

"That is just what I wanted you to say," the Lord Chamberlain enthused. "Now let's go and talk to the man who I know is an experienced and brilliant actor."

Remembering how Michael had related that he had been disguised as an Indian Holy Man and a native horse-dealer, she was sure that the Lord Chamberlain was right.

She then followed him into Michael's room where he was sitting up in bed enjoying his breakfast.

"Good morning," he called out to them cheerfully, "I was not expecting such early visitors."

"I have a job for you to do," the Lord Chamberlain answered, "and I feel that only *you* can carry it off."

"Since you are obviously flattering me, I am quite sure it is going to be a difficult one!"

The Lord Chamberlain told him all he had just told Narina and he listened intently.

Then the Lord Chamberlain continued,

"Prince Hans has said that he will leave us after the Parade and since the sooner we are rid of him the better, I have ordered it to take place at half-past one.

"Luncheon will be early but as you will understand, I want to see the back of Prince von Vechtel as speedily as possible."

"So do I," agreed Michael, "but you will certainly make me pay for my supper!"

"I am sure you will do it brilliantly," added Narina.

"I only hope that Prince Rudolf's uniform will fit me. If there is one thing I dislike it is looking unsmart and down-at-heel when I am on official business."

Narina knew he was only teasing and she riposted,

"I am certain Paks will turn you out looking spick and span!"

The Lord Chamberlain walked towards the door.

"I am extremely grateful to you both," he said, "and I can only hope that Prince Hans will not be too scornful about our Army. We all know only too well what would be the consequence of that."

He left the room before either of them could reply.

Then Narina turned to Michael,

"I feel sure you can do it and only you can make that

mischief-maker believe that the Alexanderburg Army is bigger than it really looks and is going to grow bigger in the future."

"Is that true?" asked Michael.

There was a pause before Narina replied,

"It is what the Lord Chamberlain desires, but the Prime Minister and a great number of other people here in the City prefer things exactly as they have always been and have no wish to move with the times."

"That is what I want to know. Now play your part by looking exceedingly beautiful and smart so that Prince Hans will have something much more interesting to attract his attention. We don't want him to observe that the Army is too short of men to secure the gates when the Russians are pressing to enter."

Narina gave a cry.

"Oh no! Somehow you must stop them."

"Just me?" asked Michael, mockingly.

"Why not? If you can outwit the Russians in one way, as you have done in India, then you can in another, especially for this small country which desperately needs your help."

She looked at him as she finished speaking, but he did not answer her.

As Narina walked towards her room, she knew that the Lord Chamberlain was extremely worried.

Prince Rudolf and Princess Louise had gone away confident that nothing untoward would happen while they were in Constantinople.

Yet now everything was in turmoil.

She would have liked to talk for longer to Michael and then as she had reached her sitting room, she saw Paks hurrying into the State bedroom.

She had nothing to do but go back to her room and so she then began changing the dress she was wearing for something more spectacular.

Next she chose a matching hat to go with it, which was decorated with ostrich feathers.

Maria came into the room and exclaimed,

"Why didn't you ring for me, Lady? I've only just heard that the Army's to be inspected."

"I was looking to see what I should wear, Maria, because I am sure there will be a large crowd."

"You can be sure of that, Lady, there'll be no one in the City today. They'll all be on the ground outside where our Army be on parade."

She spoke proudly and Narina could only hope the people watching would feel proud of their Army too.

Maria brought her some of Louise's jewellery.

When she opened the jewel box, Narina saw to her surprise that inside it was a small revolver.

"Where did this come from?" she asked Maria.

"It's what Her Royal Highness always carries when she goes outside the City. His Royal Highness insists on it, and although she's never had to use it as yet, I always puts it ready for her as he instructed me."

"Then I will take it too," declared Narina firmly.

Her dear father had taught her to shoot when she was young and she had often carried a pistol or a revolver when they travelled abroad.

This one was very small and exquisitely enamelled, besides having Louise's initials in diamonds on it.

"His Royal Highness gives it to her as soon as they were married," Maria said as if she had asked the question. "I always says if it can kill someone, it'd be a pretty way of dying!"

"That's one way of looking at it," smiled Narina.

She put the revolver in the pocket of her gown and although it was rather heavy at her side, she felt that it was somehow comforting.

Luncheon was punctual at twelve-thirty, but when they sat down there was no sign of Michael.

As if someone had asked him the question, the Lord Chamberlain explained,

"His Royal Highness is intending to go straight to the Parade, which I think is wise. It would be a mistake on his first day out of his bed for him to do too much and it is important he should use his eyes as little as possible."

Prince Hans did not seem particularly interested.

Once again he was paying Narina compliments, but she did not feel that they were as intense or sincere as they had been last evening.

Even now she found it hard to believe that he had actually dared to steal the key and come to her room.

When she had told Maria that it was missing, she had given a little cry of horror.

"How could that have happened?" she asked. "Are you suggesting that someone has taken it?"

"I really don't know, Maria, I am only aware that it was not in the lock as it had been the previous night."

After breakfast when she went to change her gown, Maria announced triumphantly that she had found the key.

"It had fallen on the mat just outside the door," she said. "I cannot think how it got there and no one noticed it as the mat's made of thick wool and the key's very small."

Narina felt certain that Prince Hans had deliberately dropped it there, but it would be a mistake to say so.

*

Luncheon was over two minutes after one o'clock.

A large carriage was waiting with a Cavalry escort to convey Narina, Prince Hans and the Lord Chamberlain to the Royal Parade ground.

As they drove through the City, Narina thought that the streets looked remarkably empty and then she realised that practically everyone had gone to see the Parade.

When they arrived, a Regimental Band was playing beside a platform decorated with flowers.

A large number of soldiers were already in position in what seemed to Narina the most enormous field she had ever seen.

Growing round it on all sides were wild flowers no less beautiful than those planted in the garden and equally beautiful were the flowering bushes and trees.

Because the scene was so attractive, it almost hurt her to see that the Cavalry had trampled down some of the wild flowers.

When their carriage came to a standstill, there was a horse waiting for Prince Hans.

As he was about to mount it, Michael appeared.

He looked so entirely different that for a moment Narina felt that it could not be him.

He was wearing the feathered hat of a General and his dazzling red uniform was covered with decorations and round his neck hung the golden star of Alexanderburg.

He was mounted on a magnificent white horse and looked really splendid and exactly as the leader of a Royal Army should look.

As he rode into the Parade ground, the crowds of people who had come from the City waved and cheered.

The women curtsied low and the men bowed their heads.

Michael acknowledged them all gracefully with a wave from a white-gloved hand.

Then he rode over to where Prince Hans was just mounting the horse provided for him and the two of them started to ride up and down the ranks.

Narina was not surprised that the people watching were excited.

The Band was playing and the Prime Minister and the whole Cabinet were already on the platform as Narina and the Lord Chamberlain sat down in the front row.

The two empty chairs beside them were for Prince Rudolf and his guest Prince Hans when the inspection was finished.

It did not take long as there were not a vast number of soldiers on Parade.

They rode back and climbed onto the platform and everyone rose to their feet.

As the two Princes walked across to their chairs the women curtsied again and it was then for the first time the band stopped playing.

Michael, as Prince Rudolf, walked to the front of the platform.

The trumpets sounded to ensure silence.

Then much to Narina's surprise, Michael called out in a voice that rang out over the Parade ground,

"I want everyone to come as near as possible to the platform so that they can hear what I have to say."

He must already have given orders to the soldiers, who marched forward so that they were much closer.

The crowd were then directed to move as near as possible on each side of them.

As this was all happening, Michael stood watching them and waiting.

He had his back to the Prime Minister and members of the Cabinet who would know Prince Rudolf by sight.

When it seemed that everyone was still and ready to listen, he raised his voice.

Speaking slowly but very loudly he began,

"You have all come here today to welcome Prince Hans von Vechtel, who has asked specially if he can meet our Army. He has, I am certain, been impressed by your smartness and the excellent turnout that he and I have just witnessed."

There were cheers at this from the crowd.

"Now I want to take this opportunity of talking to you about the future. First of all I want to explain to you how sorry I am that I have not been able for the past week or so to make any contact with you because of my injury."

Narina saw that the people were listening intently.

"You have been told that I had a fall out riding, but actually that was untrue. I was assaulted by some strange men who I am certain did not come from Alexanderburg. They would have kidnapped or killed me, if I had not been able to fight them off."

There was a murmur of horror from the audience.

Narina wondered why he was saying all this.

"What happened then has now convinced me that we have to enlarge our Army immediately. I am hoping every able-bodied man and boy in the country will enlist and serve for long enough as a soldier to be trained to fight for our freedom in the future should it ever be necessary."

There was a loud murmur when he paused.

"I intend to have the most up-to-date weapons for my Army, especially modern guns which have a far longer range and are more accurate than those we have used in the past. It will require much intelligence and determination to handle them, but I am certain that is something we have plenty of amongst my people."

There were cheers and Narina could see the faces of the young men listening light up.

"I expect some of you are wondering how we can afford a much larger Army than we have already, equipped with much more up-to-date and expensive weapons.

"I am sure all the women are calculating that they may have to give up the pretty gowns they want or, more important, the food their family needs. There will however be no need for any sacrifices on the part of the people of Alexanderburg, and I will tell you why."

There was absolute silence and expectation.

"It is in fact my clever wife's idea and I know it is something that you will all enjoy. Where you are standing at this moment and stretching out as far as you can see, we will create a playground or if you prefer it a vast 'Pleasure Garden', which will attract visitors from all over the world because it will be so beautiful."

There was an audible gasp from his audience.

"There will be near to it – and this is where some of you who are too old to join the Army will be working – a large Rifle Range where everyone from the smallest child can learn to shoot.

"In the Alexanderburg Pleasure Garden there will be bowling alleys, swings for the children and many other amusements. Now listen for the most significant of all."

The crowd seemed to hold their breath.

"Every village and town in the country will have its own Public Garden. They will compete with each other to win medals and prizes for the best or most original display. We will bring in plants from the Himalayas, China, Nepal and many other countries."

Now the people were wide-eyed and he finished triumphantly,

"I assure you we will be a show place for the whole of Europe and we will need to enlarge our Port to take in the ships that will bring visitors up from the Mediterranean to see all that is unique in Alexanderburg."

There was silence.

Then the people who had been listening as if they were afraid to miss one word opened their mouths to shout.

Michael threw out his arms saying,

"*Will you do it*? *Can you do it*? Are all of us clever enough to challenge Europe and the world with our exotic gardens of many amusements?"

There was a shriek, a cry, and the cheers seemed to rise up into the sky and become almost deafening.

The soldiers were cheering too.

Michael turned and taking Narina by the hand drew her to her feet.

It was impossible for either of them to speak above the roar of the crowd.

He stood with an arm round her shoulders and both of them waved with their free hands.

Finally at a signal from Michael the Band played the National Anthem and everyone on the platform rose to their feet and they all sang passionately.

The inspirational sound of their voices seemed to Narina to portray their pride and love for their country.

Only as the Band finished playing and the cheering began again did Michael take Narina across the platform.

They walked down the steps to where the carriage was waiting for them and Michael helped her into it and Prince Hans joined her.

Then as the Lord Chamberlain took his seat and the carriage started off, Narina saw Michael riding away.

He was on his white stallion followed by a General and other Officers. They left the soldiers to relax and talk to the excited crowd of citizens.

As they entered the City, Prince Hans exclaimed,

"I must admit, Your Royal Highness, that I had no idea that your husband was such a good speaker or that he would spring such a surprise on us as he has just done."

"I was surprised myself," agreed Narina. "But the flowers here are so beautiful, I am sure people will want to come from other countries to view them."

"And, of course, they will," the Lord Chamberlain cried. "I cannot imagine why we have not thought of this before. I think we should be very grateful to Prince Hans, because it is his visit that has triggered off what I am quite certain is going to lead to a transformation of this country into a prosperity it has never known before."

"I am really delighted," Prince Hans replied, "and if in any way I have had a hand in waking up your political leaders, then it is something I must try to achieve in other countries as well!"

From the way he spoke Narina was certain that he would take all the credit. However, it would be excellent for him to inform the outside world and far more exciting than if its Army was too small to protect the country.

They arrived back at the Palace, but there was no sign of Michael.

Narina wondered how long he would be before he joined them as she was worried that he had done too much.

He might be feeling limp and exhausted as he had been on the first day after his arrival.

The servants were arranging for tea to be served in one of the reception rooms.

She went out of the door into the garden, thinking perhaps Michael had left his horse at the stables and that he would walk back amongst the flowers as she loved to do.

She reached the fountain.

And then she saw a feathered hat coming through the bushes on one side of the garden.

Michael was walking through the lilies, which were showing white and pure against his bright red coat.

Then just before he reached her, she saw a man rise from behind a thick bush covered in blossom.

He pointed a shotgun at Michael.

Michael had his back towards the man as he walked to the Palace and had no idea that he was in any danger.

Before the assassin could take aim, Narina drew the small revolver from her pocket.

With a swiftness and accuracy which would have delighted her father she shot the man in the shoulder.

At the report of her revolver, Michael then stopped, turned round and realised what was happening.

As the sentries guarding the Palace grounds came running into the garden, he took the revolver from Narina's hand and urged her,

"Go into the house now, my darling! I don't want you mixed up in this turmoil."

For a moment Narina hesitated.

Then realising the sentries had seized the man, who was screaming with pain, she did as she was told.

She saw as she reached the entrance that an equerry was waiting there with the Prime Minister, who had come to tea having no idea of what had just happened.

Without speaking to either of them, she ran up the stairs and into her bedroom.

As she slumped down into a chair by the dressing table, she could only think that she had saved Michael.

If she had not taken the revolver with her, he might at this very moment be dead.

She felt her whole being cry out with horror,

But he was alive and she had saved him.

And if she had not been able to do so, she would have lost someone, who, strange as it might seem, she now knew meant very much to her.

She did not ring at once for Maria, but a little later she came bustling in.

"What on earth can be going on here, what's the to-do downstairs?" she asked. "They says that someone tried to shoot His Royal Highness and you, Lady, saved him."

"It was you who saved him, Maria. You told me to take the revolver and, if I had not done so, that man would have undoubtedly killed our patient from next door."

"Well, thank God it didn't happen, Lady, I were so afraid that someone might guess that Prince Rudolf be not who he appears to be."

Maria dropped her voice on the last words and even as she spoke, the door opened and Michael came in.

Narina jumped to her feet.

"You are all right? You are not hurt?" she asked him anxiously.

"Only because you were clever and brave enough to save me. It is most important that the people chattering downstairs and making a noise like a peacock's pen should not get a closer look at me."

Narina smiled.

"Go into your bedroom," she suggested. "I am sure that Paks will keep them out."

Michael crossed the room rapidly and opened the communicating-door.

Narina heard him speaking and was sure that Paks must have been waiting for him.

"He'll be all right," Maria added, as if she realised Narina was worried. "And they'll be talking too much of what's happened to have noticed any difference between him and His Royal Highness."

"I hope you are right, Maria, it was just unfortunate that the man was waiting for him so close to the Palace."

"If you asks me, them sentries aren't doing their job as well as they should."

Narina thought the same, but realised that it would be meaningless to say so.

She merely took off her hat and tidied herself.

Then she knocked on the communicating-door and Michael called out for her to come in.

She entered to find the room darkened as it usually was and Michael was already in bed.

"It is only me," Narina breathed.

"You are the one person I now wish to see – and no others. Keep them all out, Paks."

"I'll do that right enough for you," Paks muttered. "But you've given them a lot to gossip about and you can bet your last penny they'll want to come here and talk and talk about it to you."

"Then they are not going to do so. In fact, as I am feeling so ill, the only person allowed to see me now is Her Royal Highness."

Paks grinned.

"Leave it to me then and I'm a much better guard than them soldiers who gives themselves such airs."

He walked from the room, Narina laughed and then she asked Michael,

"Who is the man who was trying to kill you?"

"I think he must be part of a separate Russian plot to assassinate Prince Rudolf and create a vacuum for them to walk into. But there is no point in discussing it now. I want to tell you just how wonderful I think you are and how brilliantly you saved my life. Who taught you to shoot as well as that?"

"My father – and he will be so delighted that I was able to protect you as he taught me to protect myself."

"How can you look like you do and be so accurate with a firearm?" quizzed Michael.

Narina chuckled.

"It sounds so funny when you say it like that, but I have always believed in being a 'Jack of all trades', and I have most certainly tried some new trades here that I never anticipated would come anywhere near my life!"

"What did you think of my speech, Narina?"

"You were really brilliant and it was exactly what was needed. Above all you gave Prince Hans something different to think about other than he intended."

"I was well aware of what he intended and it would have been totally disastrous. Now the Russians will find it impossible to get any of the Alexanderburg people to listen to them when they try to stir up trouble.

"And unless Prince Rudolf on his return reverses all I have suggested, I am very certain that Alexanderburg will become a boom-town and thousands of tourists will flock in year after year."

"I pray you are right and I can only hope that Prince Rudolf will carry out your ideas as stringently as you have thought them out yourself."

"He can hardly expect me to remain here and just organise a Pleasure Garden. In point of fact, as it happens, there are a great number of other things I would very much like to discuss with you."

Narina felt a thrill of excitement go through her.

"Oh, *please* tell me about your ideas, Michael."

At that moment the door opened.

"The Lord Chamberlain is here to see Your Royal Highness," announced Paks.

He entered the room and walked towards the bed.

"Are you all right?" he asked Michael.

"I have survived a rather alarming experience, Lord Chamberlain, but I am totally unscathed thanks entirely to Narina."

"I am aware of her unbelievable bravery," said the Lord Chamberlain, "and I do not know how to thank her."

He paused for a moment before he added,

"Well, I have news for both of you that is of great significance and I only hope that you, Michael, are not too tired to hear it."

The Lord Chamberlain looked down at a piece of paper he held in his hand.

Almost as if he was frightened of his own voice, the Lord Chamberlain looked over his shoulder before he sat down in a chair beside the bed.

"I have just now received an urgent coded message from Constantinople."

"From Louise?" Narina asked. "Has anything gone wrong?"

The Lord Chamberlain shook his head.

"No, nothing has gone wrong. In fact the operation has been a complete success and Their Royal Highnesses are returning tonight!"

Narina stared at him.

"*Tonight*," she said in a voice he could hardly hear.

"The message they have sent me is in a code, which only I know. It informs me that they are arriving tonight and landing at the Summer Palace, where you, Narina, are to meet them."

He was silent for a moment before carrying on,

"Naturally they have no idea that Michael is here, but it is essential that he should go with you and that you both should leave on the same Battleship that brought you here from London."

Narina thought miserably that this was the end.

It was just what she had anticipated, when she had realised without being told that it would be impossible for her to stay in Alexanderburg once Louise had returned.

Naturally that now concerned Michael as well and it flashed through her mind that he might want to return to India.

"So we have to leave this evening," said Michael in a quiet controlled voice.

"I am afraid so. We cannot risk anyone seeing you together and it was astute of His Royal Highness to think of the Summer Palace."

No one spoke and he continued,

"I was thinking on my way up here that it would be best for me to announce that His Royal Highness has gone there for a few days' rest after the terrible shock of being nearly killed after the Parade – and his wife is by his side."

"Do you really think I must leave at once?" Narina asked. "I did want to spend a little time with Louise."

"I think under the present circumstances it would be a grave mistake. We have not only had Prince Hans nosing about to find out our secrets, but there will now be a real host of busy-bodies wanting to discuss with His Royal Highness the various ideas you have both put forward, for which I am extremely grateful."

"I thought you would be. It was really your being so depressed over the situation and Narina's interest in the flowers that made the idea come to me."

"You are the sort of man that every country needs at this moment, especially those in the Balkans. I only wish by some magical way we could keep you here. But I think we can make you a promise that you will both come back next year or the year after. Also it would be only right for Her Royal Highness to ask you to be Godparents to the heir to the throne who I am very certain will now be the result of their visit to Constantinople."

"I have been praying that it would be," said Narina.

"I am sure your prayers will be answered."

"How soon do you want us to go?" Michael asked the Lord Chamberlain.

"I think that you should leave as soon as it is dark. The only question is whether you would prefer to travel on horseback or in a carriage driven by Paks."

He looked at Narina and then at Michael and added,

"You do understand that the only two people who can go with you are Paks to valet His Royal Highness as he always does and Maria to maid Princess Louise."

"I personally would wish to ride," replied Michael. "And I know where the Summer Palace is because I passed it when I was coming here to be saved by Narina."

"And I too would rather ride than anything else," concurred Narina. "It is the one thing I have missed and it had been sheer agony seeing those magnificent horses in the stables and not being able to ride any of them!"

"It will not take you long and I suggest you have

something to eat and drink before you go, although there are servants in the Summer Palace who will be providing supper for Their Royal Highnesses when they arrive."

"Do the servants know that they have travelled to Constantinople?"

"No, of course not, they will think they have merely been inspecting the Battleship and it will be of no interest to them that two people who have been staying here in the Palace should leave Alexanderburg by sea."

Narina laughed.

"I see you have it all beautifully worked out, Lord Chamberlain, and I must certainly congratulate you on the way you have managed to keep our secret so well, although I thought several times it would prove impossible."

"Cross your fingers tightly till you actually leave," replied the Lord Chamberlain. "I can only thank you both for everything you have done and insist that it was not only a magnificent effort but a triumphant victory!"

"That is just what we feel ourselves, and I warn you I intend to come back next year and see if you have carried out my ideas. I shall be disappointed if you have not!"

"As they are just what was required for our country and as the Prime Minister believes that it is Prince Rudolf himself who has suggested them, it is going to be seriously difficult for anyone not to do as they are told."

Narina clasped her hands together and cried,

"I am glad, so very *very* glad."

"I am going to send you up a bottle of the very best champagne," said the Lord Chamberlain, rising to his feet, "and I will come back to talk to you before you leave. But now I must go downstairs and assure them that His Royal Highness is fine but a little shocked by his experience and I can say the same of Her Royal Highness as well."

Before he closed the door he looked back,

"Thank you, thank you both again, you have been magnificent. There is no other word for it."

And then he was gone.

Narina gave a little laugh.

"Well at least we made one person happy. I can see how frustrating it has been for the Lord Chamberlain until now when everything that he has suggested has either been turned down or ignored."

"I think it is people-power that will do it," Michael added, "they were all entranced by the idea of the Pleasure Garden and I'm sure that the young men of Alexanderburg have all been wanting for a long time to join the Army."

"The Rifle Range was a very good idea, and that in itself will make them keen."

"I hope they will be good shots like you, Narina!"

"I don't want to think about it, but if Maria had not shown me the revolver and told me that Louise had always carried it in her pocket when outside the City, we might not be talking to each other at this moment."

"Would that have worried you?"

Michael spoke very quietly.

And it seemed to Narina that the answer she should give him was being repeated loudly in her mind and in her heart.

CHAPTER SEVEN

The horses were ready.

They had been brought round to a side door where Paks took them over, which meant that no one saw Narina and Michael off.

She had spoken to Maria and told her not to forget any of her belongings or to pack by mistake those that were Louise's.

Maria did point out that she had not yet unpacked any of her clothes!

As Narina walked slowly downstairs, she knew that she was miserable at having to leave and so abruptly.

She had been so happy at the Palace and it was sad to think that she must leave now and perhaps never see it again.

Then she told herself she was being unnecessarily sensitive and, of course, she would return one day.

But she realised that what really saddened her was the thought that if she did come back, Michael would not be here.

When he appeared in a very smart riding jacket that belonged to Prince Rudolf, he was looking very handsome.

There was a sudden agony in her heart because she had to leave him behind.

He would return to India where he was needed and perhaps be killed because she was not there to protect him.

She wanted to beg him to come to England where he would be safe, but he would only laugh at her and tell her how much he enjoyed the adventure and excitement of *The Great Game.*

Michael lifted her up gently onto the side saddle of her mount and once again she felt that strange feeling she had felt before at his touch.

She really could not explain it to herself, but it was something which was half agony and half ecstasy.

"I will see you later, Paks," Michael called out as they rode off.

It was already dusk and the first stars were coming out in the sky.

As the Lord Chamberlain had suggested, they had had already eaten and had drunk the delicious champagne he had so kindly provided for them.

Narina could not help thinking that she must talk to Louise and stay for an hour at least at the Summer Palace.

It was only as they were both riding away that she suddenly remembered that they had not said goodbye to the Lord Chamberlain.

She had been so bemused talking with Michael and drinking champagne that she had not been able to think of anything else.

Now she turned to him, half reining in her mount,

"We didn't say goodbye to the Lord Chamberlain!"

"I know, Narina, because he has changed his mind at the last moment. As we are riding there, he is driving with Paks and Maria to the Summer Palace."

Narina gave a sigh of relief.

She had no wish to seem in any way rude to a man who had been so considerate to her ever since her arrival.

Secretly she thought if he was going to the Summer Palace, he would be able to tell Prince Rudolf better than Michael could what had been arranged for him and Louise in their absence.

They rode for a little while in silence.

Now the full moon was rising high in the sky and the stars were growing brighter by the second.

"It's so lovely here," sighed Narina to Michael, "I really don't want to go away."

"England can be lovely too, you know, Narina."

She agreed and nothing was more glorious than the garden at her home and she was always riding in the woods alone except when her father found the time to join her.

But there would be no one for her to talk to as she had been able to talk to Michael.

*

They rode on.

Now they were near the sea and the moonlight was glittering on the waves as they rolled in below them.

Then to her surprise Michael suggested,

"We will now turn to the left here at this wood and I would like you to follow me, please."

"But surely the Summer Palace is right on the sea," murmured Narina.

"I am taking you somewhere else first – "

She was surprised but obviously there was no hurry.

Paks was driving a slow old-fashioned carriage and he would have to stay on the road that ran along the top of the cliff.

And anyway riding as they were on soft ground, it seemed better to delay their arrival for a little while so that the Lord Chamberlain arrived before them.

It was very dark in the wood and, as woods always did, it felt an enchanted place to Narina.

Impulsively she exclaimed,

"When I ride out in the woods at home, which I do every day, I have always wished there was someone with me who felt the same as I do."

"I feel the same as you do," replied Michael. "And that is why I have brought you this way – "

"You love gardens and flowers. I thought therefore you must love the little red squirrels that climb up the trees, and the goblins and hobgoblins who live beneath them."

"I used to listen to them when I was a small boy."

"I guessed that you did, Michael, and I have always been absolutely certain there are water nymphs in the little pool in the wood and I used to sit by the water often and watch and watch hoping that one would pop out."

"I think one did come out for me," sighed Michael. "But when I saw her in the sunlight, she turned out to be an angel!"

Narina blushed in the darkness, but she knew that he meant that she had saved his life and she said quickly,

"You must be careful when I am not around. After all it was chance or perhaps the hand of God that I was looking for you in the garden and – "

"Please forget it!" Michael cried, interrupting her. "I really don't want you to dwell on what happened then. You saved my life twice – and there must not be a third."

"That is what I am trying to make you understand," replied Narina. "If I am not there, those dreadful men who have been pursuing you may *still* catch up with you."

There was a note of horror in her voice.

She thought that Michael was going to reply to her, but instead he quickened his pace a little.

Now he was riding ahead of her.

As the track through the wood was dark and narrow it seemed sensible to ride in single file.

At the same time it was strange that he wanted to ride through the trees when they would be able to see more clearly outside on the cliff.

Then she suddenly felt afraid that there might be an enemy lurking ahead and he was unaware of any danger.

She wanted to call out to him to be very careful and to let her go first – just in case there was someone hiding behind the trees.

Then unexpectedly just in front of them she saw a clearing.

And at the far side of it there was a small building that appeared to be a Chapel.

Michael had drawn in his horse so that she could come up beside him.

As she did so, Narina remarked,

"It is an ancient Chapel built in the very middle of the wood. How fascinating!"

"I thought you would think so, Narina, and that is why I have brought you here."

"Do you mean we can go inside?"

"It is a Chapel belonging to an old Priest, who has retired here because he loved the woods as we love them. He feeds the rabbits and the squirrels. The wild stags come here too in the evening because he has tamed them with his love of nature."

Narina was listening to him entranced.

Then to her surprise Michael dismounted.

"Are we going inside?" she asked him.

"I am going to introduce you to the Priest. He was very kind recently to me on my way to the City."

"Oh, I would love to meet him."

Michael lifted Narina to the ground.

Then he fastened both horses' bridles to a wooden fence that was obviously for people who visited the Priest on horseback.

Narina stood looking round her, then up at the stars peeping down overhead.

"I have brought you here, my very precious angel," Michael declared, "*so that we can be married*."

For a moment Narina felt she could not have heard him right.

"To be married?" she asked incoherently.

"You have saved my life twice, my darling Narina. Therefore, as the old legend goes, I am your responsibility for life. So you now have to look after me and protect me, and that is what I desire more than I have ever wished for anything before in my whole life."

Narina gazed at him and she could not speak.

She only thought that what she was hearing could not be true.

It must all be part of a dream.

Then Michael added more softly,

"I love you, Narina, and I believe you love me. We will talk about it later, but let us now be married so that I can be absolutely sure of *never* losing you."

He took Narina's hands as he was speaking.

He drew her up the entrance steps and through the door of the Chapel which was ajar.

There were six candles alight on the altar.

The old Priest, wearing his vestments, was kneeling in prayer on the steps.

As Narina and Michael entered, there was a flutter of wings from many birds, perching above the altar and on the windowsills at the side of the Chapel.

As they walked towards the Priest, Narina saw that there were rabbits and squirrels peeping out from behind the altar itself.

They were completely unafraid, only curious as to why they were there.

The old Priest must have heard their footsteps and he rose from his knees and as he turned round, he smiled when he saw Michael.

"You promised me you would return, my son, and I have been praying that all has gone well with you."

"All your prayers have saved me, Father, and I was sent by the mercy of God someone else who has saved my life – not once but twice."

The Priest turned to Narina,

"I welcome you, my child, to this Chapel and I feel sure that you will feel the hand of God is here to help you at any time you should need it – "

"What I need at this moment," Michael said before Narina could say another word, "is that you should please marry us *now*."

The old Priest was obviously delighted.

"Nothing will give me greater pleasure and I know without you telling me that you will receive and give each other the true love that comes only from God."

Michael took Narina's hand in his.

The Priest turned first to the altar where he prayed and crossed himself, then turned back to them.

Without further ado, he then started the Marriage Service.

He said it simply but with a sincerity that seemed in itself to be more Holy than anything Narina had ever heard in her life before.

When they arrived at the point when Narina was to receive the ring, she wondered what Michael would do.

Much to her surprise he took a ring from the pocket of his riding jacket.

After the Priest had blessed the ring he put it on her finger gently and carefully and she saw that it was a plain gold ring with just one large ruby embedded in the gold.

She guessed it must be Michael's signet ring and it fitted her finger perfectly.

The Priest named them man and wife and they knelt for his final Blessing.

Narina was totally convinced that all the angels and archangels of Heaven were singing overhead.

Her beloved mother was looking down on her and was feeling happy that she had found someone to love and who really loved her.

Finally the Priest sprinkled both of them with Holy Water and then he knelt again in front of the altar.

Narina was praying that she would make Michael happy and that he would never regret having married her in such a strange way.

He put out his hand to draw her to her feet and then took her to the door of the Chapel and opened it.

Before they went down the steps he closed the door behind them.

Only as they reached the horses did Narina suggest,

"Should we say goodbye and thank him?

Michael shook his head.

"I knew that he would be here when I needed him, because he told me he always prays at night. As you saw the birds, the rabbits and the squirrels pray with him."

"It was sublimely wonderful, yet somehow it seems unreal. Am I really your wife, Michael?"

"I intend to convince you I am your husband and it was not just a dream, but at the moment I feel we are flying up into the sky and I only want to think of you and nothing else."

He did not kiss her as she thought he would do, but lifted her onto her horse.

And then he mounted his own and they rode slowly back out of the wood.

When they were outside and the moon was shining down on them and they could again see the silver sea in its light, Narina asked herself once more if it was really true.

Could it in any way be possible that she was now married to Michael without his first asking her if she would be his wife?

Yet the ring was now firmly on her finger and the old Priest had said all the words of the Marriage Service to them.

She gazed at the ring and then at Michael as he was riding beside her.

She was quite certain that she must be dreaming.

When she woke up, it would only be what she had wished for and not really what had happened.

As if he knew what she was thinking Michael said,

"I will answer your questions, my darling Narina, later tonight when we are alone. But first we have to meet with Louise and Rudolf who we have been impersonating, and then we will be able to be ourselves without feeling we are acting a part."

As he spoke Narina thought of what she had always been told – that if you wanted to act well, you had to think yourself into believing that you really were the person you were impersonating.

That was why Michael was determined they would no longer be pretending to be anyone else but themselves.

'Only he could think of that,' she mused and it made him fit even more easily into her private world.

She had read of it in legends and fairy stories until she had imagined herself part of them.

In the future she would not have to imagine she was anyone else and would be herself with someone she loved and who loved her.

They would be a part of each other.

She knew now that Michael was the companion she had longed for in the woods at home, who she thought she would never find.

As they rode on in silence, she felt certain that his heart was beating the same way as hers.

They were riding into a perfect happiness which no one would ever be able to take away from them.

*

Ahead of her Narina could now see the walls of the Summer Palace shimmering in the bright moonlight.

It was not very large but it was beautifully designed and looked somehow in the distance like a Greek Temple.

When they drew nearer she saw that the garden was ablaze with banks of beautiful flowers and the Royal flag of Alexanderburg was flying proudly on the roof.

As they rode in through the gate which led up to the Palace, Narina could see there were two grooms waiting to take their horses.

She realised that the carriage must have arrived in front of them and then the Lord Chamberlain had informed them that they were not far behind.

The front door was open and servants were waiting to welcome them.

She and Michael were then formally escorted into a beautifully decorated room that overlooked the sea.

There was a cry of delight from Louise.

She jumped up from the sofa where she was sitting beside Prince Rudolf and ran towards Narina.

"Dearest Narina!" she cried. "You have come and I am so glad to see you. We were just beginning to wonder what had detained you. We were a little afraid in case you had suffered an accident – "

"We stopped for a while at the little Chapel in the woods," Narina explained when she could speak.

"Oh, it is so enchanting," enthused Louise. "But I had no idea that you would go there."

"Anyway you are now here," added Prince Rudolf, "and I want to tell you just how grateful I am not only to you but to Mr. Ward. The Lord Chamberlain has told me how marvellously he had impersonated me at the Parade."

Michael laughed.

"I only hope, Your Royal Highness, that I have not given you too much to do."

"The Lord Chamberlain has told us how brilliant you were in giving Prince Hans something to think about. We are both so thrilled with Narina's idea of the Pleasure Garden and only wish that we had been clever enough to think of it ourselves!"

"It will certainly keep you busy, Louise."

"I only wish you were going to be here to help me, Narina, but alas, dearest, you must leave this evening. The

Lord Chamberlain is terrified in case anyone finds out that we are not really as clever as the whole of Alexanderburg thinks, so when you have drunk a glass of champagne, I am afraid we shall have to say goodbye to you."

"At least I will not be going alone," sighed Narina.

She glanced at Michael as she spoke and he added,

"I think it is only correct that we should tell Your Royal Highnesses that the reason we went to the Chapel in the wood was to be married. *Narina is now my wife.*"

Louise gave a shriek of excitement.

"Oh, dearest Narina, this is wonderful!" she cried. "How thrilled your father will be!"

"I don't think he will know much about Michael, but, of course, I will tell him all about his amazing exploits in *The Great Game* in India."

Michael smiled.

"You will do nothing of the sort, Narina, that is all a secret, as you well know. But strange though it seems, one cannot help people talking."

They laughed and then Prince Rudolf chipped in,

"Maybe I should have informed you, Mr. Ward, as soon as you arrived – "

Narina and Michael looked at him, wondering what he was about to tell them.

"When we were both in Constantinople, I managed to buy a few English newspapers for Louise as she always enjoys them. *The Morning Post* is nearly a week old, but it reports the death of the Earl of Hereward, who I think must be a near relation of yours."

"He is my father!" exclaimed Michael.

"*Your father*! But it reports, and here it is, that the heir to the Earldom is Viscount Here, an *aide-de-camp* to the Viceroy of India."

Michael smiled.

"I did indeed go out to India as *aide-de-camp* to the Viceroy, but when I became immersed in *The Great Game*, I temporarily gave up my title for obvious reasons."

"I am very sorry that your father is dead," Narina murmured, "it must come as a terrible shock to you."

Michael shook his head.

"My father has been ill for a long time and I knew I would have to go home fairly soon. My brother will have seen to the funeral and arranged it all in my absence."

There was silence for a moment.

Then Prince Rudolf proposed,

"Well, as you have just been married, we cannot let you be sad or depressed at this particular moment. Let us all drink your health and hope that you and Narina will be as blissfully happy as Louise and I are."

"I will drink to that," agreed the Lord Chamberlain.

"And so will I," added Louise.

They toasted them in champagne and then Michael saw Prince Rudolf looking at the clock.

"I think that you want us to go?" he queried.

"I am sorry to seem to be inhospitable, but the Lord Chamberlain has impressed on us both how essential it is that no one should suspect for a single moment that it was not I who spoke so brilliantly at the Army Parade, or that it was not Louise's idea for the children's competition, which I know will keep every woman in Alexanderburg busy for the next two months.

"The Battleship will take you to England and there is no hurry. If you would like to stop anywhere on the way home, just tell the Captain."

"I will do that and thank you so very much, Your Royal Highness," said Michael gratefully.

Louise put her arms round Narina and whispered so that only she could hear,

"I am thrilled that you are now a Countess, dearest Narina. It will make it easier when you come back to stay with us here for a long visit and no one will suspect for a moment that you ever pretended to be me."

"I will deliberately try to look very different when I do come back!"

"And I hope by that time I will look very different too!" muttered Louise.

Narina squeezed her friend's hand.

"I am sure you will have had a baby by then and, of course, Michael and I would really love to be invited to his Christening."

"You must – and we will wait until you can come."

Narina was kissed goodbye on the cheek by Prince Rudolf and the Lord Chamberlain did the same.

"I will miss you both," he said, "but you have left me so busy that I will have no time to think about myself!"

"You must write to me and tell us everything that is happening," insisted Narina.

"Of course, I will," promised Louise.

Then they bid farewell to Paks and Maria who were waiting outside the room.

"I've put all your luggage aboard," said Paks, "and I've packed his Lordship with enough clothes of His Royal Highness's to keep him warm till he gets home."

"I am afraid I am robbing you," Michael turned to Prince Rudolf.

"I am only thankful I can give you something you really need and we will now think of something suitable as a wedding present which I promise will arrive later."

Narina thanked Prince Rudolf and Louise and then she and Michael gave tips to Paks and Maria of enough to open their eyes in surprise and they were almost incoherent in their thanks.

Then they ran as fast as they could down the Palace steps to the quayside to where a small boat was waiting for them.

As soon as they were aboard, the seamen started to row the boat rapidly to where the Battleship was anchored in the moonlight.

Both Narina and Michael waved until they were too far to be seen any longer.

Then as Narina slipped her hand into Michael's, she sighed,

"We are now saying goodbye not only to them but to Alexanderburg itself. But we *will* come back."

"Yes, we will, my darling, but I warn you there is a great deal to be done in England and you will have to help me take my father's place and there will be a large number of relatives who will be keen to meet you and who will be delighted I have married your father's daughter."

Narina laughed.

"At least it sounds respectable."

"I thought of that myself, but in fact I have married you for a great number of other reasons. And now I shall have a chance to tell you about them."

As he spoke, they arrived at the Battleship and the Captain was waiting to greet them.

"It is very nice to see you again, Miss Kenwin," he said to Narina, "and I am delighted, sir, to welcome you aboard as well."

"I think that you must be told, Captain, that Miss Kenwin and I were married this evening and I have just learnt of my father's death which means I am now the Earl of Hereward."

Marina could see that the Captain felt bewildered as to whether he should offer congratulations or condolences! Somehow he managed to convey both with some dignity.

As they went into the Saloon, he suggested,

"I think perhaps it would be more appropriate, as it is so late, to celebrate your marriage tomorrow, my Lord."

"Certainly," he agreed. "I understand it is usual for the whole crew to drink our health and that can easily be done tomorrow evening."

"Thank you, my Lord. It will be a delightful way to start our voyage back to England. I know everyone will drink yours and your wife's health with great enthusiasm."

As they were talking, the engines were beginning to turn and the Battleship began to move out to sea.

"I am just going to sail a little way down the coast," the Captain explained, "but I do not intend to pass through the Bosporus until early tomorrow morning. There is a bay nearby where I will anchor for the night."

"My wife and I would very much appreciate that," replied Michael.

When they went below, they found that two cabins had been made ready for them.

The Captain's cabin had been used by Their Royal Highnesses on their way to and from Constantinople.

This cabin boasted a large four-poster bed that was usually used by the Captain. It opened out into the sitting room Narina had used on her way to Alexanderburg.

"I am sorry we are turning you out of your cabin," Michael said politely to the Captain.

"I did so for Princess Louise and because she was so

comfortable, she asked me to give it to her friend and I find it impossible to refuse her!"

Michael chuckled.

"I am sorry you have been inconvenienced, but it is certainly exactly what we would like at this moment."

"I understand, my Lord," smiled the Captain.

*

All their luggage was carried in and Michael's case was put in the cabin next door.

For the first time since arriving in Alexanderburg, Narina took out some of her own clothes and hung them up in the wardrobe.

She realised that there was no hurry as there would be plenty of time on the voyage to unpack and repack.

She then selected her very prettiest nightgown and having washed and brushed her hair, she climbed into the four-poster bed.

She could hear voices in the next cabin and knew that one of the Stewards was unpacking Michael's clothes and doubtless assisting him as Paks had done so ably.

As the Battleship began to move faster through the water, she heard the door open.

Michael came into the cabin.

In the candlelight he seemed very tall.

Then she realised it was because he had on Prince Rudolf's long velvet robe he had worn when hiding in his bedroom at the Palace.

He closed the cabin door, then sat down on the bed.

"You look so lovely," he sighed, "so beautiful that I am asking myself if I have really been lucky enough to find anyone so perfect."

"I hope you will always think so, Michael, because everything that has happened to us has been so unreal and so enthralling that I am now afraid that when we get back to England, you will be bored."

He did not answer her question and then asked her,

"Do you realise I have not yet kissed you, Narina?"

"I felt perhaps you would after we were married," Narina replied innocently.

"I wanted to kiss you from the very first moment I saw you and you had saved my life. I knew you were more beautiful and intelligent than any woman I had ever met. But it was not only that, it was your exquisite purity that held me at bay until I found myself in a position to offer you not only my admiration but my heart and soul as well."

He was speaking in a deep voice and Narina asked,

"Is that really how you feel now?"

"What I feel now I really cannot put into words, my darling. I just know that you are part of me, you belong to me, and when we were married by the delightful old Priest in that Chapel, *God* gave you to me. That is what I have always sought and believed that one day I would find."

"Oh, Michael, that is the most wonderful thing to say," Narina whispered.

Then very gently, almost as if he was savouring the moment, Michael put his arms round her and his lips came down on hers.

It was a very gentle and loving kiss.

Yet she knew it was for him something Holy and perfect as he gave her his heart and his soul.

For what seemed an age his lips held hers captive.

Then, as he drew away from her, he sighed,

"I love you beyond words, my darling, my precious wife. I am now going to teach you to love me so that every breath we draw and every thought we have are ours for all of Eternity."

"I believe that they are already. Oh, Michael, I was so frightened that you would go back to India and I would go home alone and never see you again."

"Did you really think that I could? I think we were brought together for some very special purpose and now in our own way we have helped to save Alexanderburg from the Russians. And who knows what work is waiting for us when we reach England?"

"Anything will be exciting if it is with you."

"It will not only be exciting, but I think, although I am not sure yet what it is, there is work for us to do which will help others and justify the happiness we ourselves are feeling."

He kissed her again.

Now his kisses were becoming possessive and more passionate.

It made her feel as if something strange, wonderful and wildly exciting was rising within her.

It was moving from her lips down into her breast.

"I love you, Michael, I adore you."

Michael rose from the bed.

He took off his robe and climbed in beside her.

He did not blow out the candles.

"You are so ethereal," he whispered, "and I cannot believe you are really mine, but I will kill *anyone* who tries to take you from me."

"But no one could, because I am yours completely and absolutely."

"Not yet quite absolutely and that, my precious one, is what I am going to teach you now. But I am so afraid of frightening you."

Narina gave a little laugh.

"How could I be frightened, Michael, when I am so happy that I feel I am flying in the sky, touching the stars and am part of the moonlight."

"That is just what I feel too – "

Then he was holding her closer and closer until he was kissing her and carried on kissing her.

Narina felt as if her whole body melted into his.

The Gates of Paradise opened for them.

They were no longer two people but one.

*

A long time later Michael murmured,

"Do you still love me, my darling wife?"

"I did not know that love could be so wonderful," Narina whispered. "And I did not know that I was capable of feeling anything so unbelievably marvellous."

"My precious, I will love you until the whole world is filled with love and that is exactly what it will always be now and in the future for us."

"But you must take great care of yourself, Michael. How could I lose you now?"

"You will never lose me, Narina, we have become part of each other and now you are really mine. Our love will last not only in this life but for many lives to come."

"Do you really believe that, Michael?"

"Of course, I believe it. I do know that I have been searching for you in a number of different bodies in some very unusual places, but you have always eluded me. Now we can *never* be separated – *never* torn apart."

"That is a marvellous way to think. Oh, Michael, you have so much to teach me and I want to love you the way you want to be loved."

"Which is the way you are loving me now and the way I love you. It is what everyone hopes for and prays for in their lives, but few are as fortunate as we are to find each other."

It passed through Narina's mind that even now at the last moment fate might have kept them apart.

Michael could have easily been killed, if not by the first assassin, then by the second one.

Then she knew that God had blessed them.

They had both survived it all.

As Michael believed, having found the perfection of their love, it would be absolutely impossible for them to lose it, whatever happened in the future.

"I love you," she repeated over and over again. "I love you, Michael."

Then as she felt his heart beating against hers, she knew that once again the Gates of Paradise were opening.

As Michael made her his, he carried her up to the sky.

The God who had blessed them was blessing them again.

Whatever happened in this world or the next they would never lose Love.